GD

Halliday

Buck Halliday was a sudden man with a gun. That's why Judge Cowper, of Shimmer Creek, hired him. The judge wanted a man named Jason Henley killed. Henley, he said, had taken over the town, lock, stock and barrel, and now he expected every other businessman to pay him protection money.

Halliday had killed men before, but he wasn't a killer for hire. Still . . . maybe he could convince Henley that it might be better for his health if he made dust and headed for some-place else.

Trouble was, Henley had more lives than a cat. And to get to him, a feller first had to go through his pet gunman, the notorious Rafe Murchison.

It appeared to Halliday that he was really going to earn his money on this job.

Halliday

Adam Brady

A Black Horse Western

ROBERT HALE

First published by Cleveland Publishing Co. Pty Ltd,
New South Wales, Australia
First published in 1967
© 2019 by Piccadilly Publishing

This edition © The Crowood Press, 2020

ISBN 978-0-7198-3091-4

The Crowood Press
The Stable Block
Crowood Lane
Ramsbury
Marlborough
Wiltshire SN8 2HR

www.bhwesterns.com

Robert Hale is an imprint
of The Crowood Press

The right of Adam Brady to be identified as
author of this work has been asserted by him
in accordance with the Copyright, Designs and
Patents Act 1988

Typeset by
Derek Doyle & Associates, Shaw Heath
Printed and bound in Great Britain by
4Bind Ltd, Stevenage, SG1 2XT

ONE

SHIMMER CREEK

Buck Halliday came out of the bottom country and made for the heat-seared slopes in search of the scant comfort of a cooling breeze.

He skirted a deep dry wash and let his sorrel pick its way across ground that was more sand and gravel than solid footing. Although the slope was a gradual incline of no more than a hundred feet, it took the trail-weary horse minutes to negotiate it. On the top, the sorrel stopped and pawed the ground as if in protest.

Halliday did not have the heart to push the exhausted animal any further. Before him was an endless stretch of treeless plain, hellish with heat, dust and desolation. There was not a single sound.

For several minutes, the rider simply sat hunched in his saddle.

Then he sighed, reached for his canteen and stepped down to the ground. His clothes were plastered to his skin. He pulled out his shirttail and gave it a shake to free the fabric from his wet body.

He uncorked his canteen and pulled his bandanna from his neck and moistened it. He stepped to the head of the horse and rubbed its nose, gums and eyes with the damp cloth, then allowed himself one sip from the canteen's warm neck.

The horse stood quietly, head down, eyes part-closed, near spent. Halliday forced himself to move around, working the cramp out of his back and legs.

He was a big man, and he left deep prints in the powdery dust. After about a quarter of an hour, he climbed back into the saddle and pushed on, heading into the updraft of heat, the glare of the sun and the emptiness.

It was halfway through the afternoon when he reached the end of the long plain and encountered another run of arid slopes. This time, he spared his horse and cut through a gully between two ragged hills.

At the end of the gully, the land dropped away to reveal a sight that instantly took the tiredness away. A town sat sprawled in the heat like a sleeping animal.

Shimmer Creek . . . the name said it all.

Surrounded by bleak and treeless hills, the town had one redeeming feature – the gleaming enticement of a river.

Close to the end of his journey now, Halliday wet the bandanna again and this time squeezed water into the sorrel's mouth, repeating the practice many times.

The horse stood still in docile gratitude and nuzzled against him, as if it, too, realized that the end was close. Halliday himself refrained from drinking. He would save the last of the warm, stale water until he was absolutely certain of what lay ahead. That was an old habit, and until now it had served him well.

He climbed back into the saddle and headed for the river. There he would wash and let his horse drink its fill and rest before going into town to meet Judge Cowper.

He had Cowper's invitation in his shirt pocket, a short note offering Halliday a thousand dollars for his services and stating in clear terms that the matter was of the utmost urgency.

Halliday had never met the judge, but he had heard of him and of his activities in the county where Cowper's name was a byword.

Many years ago, as a young attorney fresh out of law school, Cowper had personally captured notorious outlaws Ben and Curt Hackett and taken them to jail. In the absence of a higher authority, he charged them with murder and sentenced them both to hang. Following that impressive effort, Cowper was quickly appointed to the bench.

The heat was slowly going out of the day, and the salt of his sweat stung Halliday's cracked lips. The hard part was over now, with Shimmer Creek no more than four miles away and the inviting bend of the river directly in front of him.

He unsaddled his horse and stripped off his clothes with his right hand while he held the horse's bridle with the left. Then he walked waist-deep into the stream, still holding the horse so that it would not drink too fast. He scooped up water in his hands and washed the horse's back, checking for sores and finding none.

When the horse finally was willing to return to the bank, Halliday left it there with reins trailing as it cropped the sweet grass.

Now it was Halliday's turn. He returned to the water and splashed around like a delighted kid. He could feel the strength flooding back into his body as the water did its cooling work. Then he walked to his crumpled clothing and returned to the water to scrub and rinse away the dust and sweat of the long ride.

He spread the garments carefully on a flat rock in the sun and lay down beside them to rest his battered body. The sun felt good on his skin.

He let his mind wander as he listened to the quiet

around him while waiting for his clothes to dry.

When he was dressed again, he ground hitched the sorrel in a good-sized patch of grass that grew along the riverbank.

He felt better now, and he was content to wait until it was dark so that he could ride into the town without attracting unwanted attention.

He took out his gun, checked the loads and balanced it thoughtfully on the palm of his hand. It was old and heavy, but it had stood the test of time and survived many a danger. Nothing could bring him to exchange the gun for a later model. It had been just Halliday and that old gun together on all the wild trails, ever since the day he killed Red Durante and was branded a gunfighter.

Sundown came and brought a welcoming cool wind with it.

Halliday shook out the saddle blanket and wiped the leather and the saddlebags carefully with a handful of grass. He saddled up and walked the horse along the riverbank until he came to a shallow spot with a sandy bottom. He mounted and crossed there, heading away from town at first so that he could make his entrance by way of a back street.

It took him only a few minutes to find the judge's place. As the judge's letter had told him, the yard was shaded by tall elm trees and the picket fence was freshly painted.

The house faced the east side of town. It was a

plain and unpretentious building that would have been as square as a box except for the long porch.

Several horses were tied outside the fence, so Halliday left his sorrel at the end of the line. Slapping the dust from his hat, he went through the gate and made his way to the porch. He could hear voices through the open windows, and from the sound of them and the number of horses at the rail, he guessed there were a dozen or so people inside the house.

He pulled out his tobacco pouch and rolled himself a smoke, leaning back against the wall to enjoy it.

Scraps of conversation drifted out to him, but it was not until a woman's voice rose angrily above the monotonous drone of men's voices that he tuned in.

'Uncle, you must be mad, hiring a man like that. You've spent your whole life trying to tame trouble-makers. Everyone respects the way you've brought law and order to this country, and for the life of me, I just can't understand how you could—'

'We have to fight fire with fire, girl,' came a deep voice in calm reply. 'Henley has the whole town cowed, and we have no way to stop him, not on our own. Now please be quiet, Beth. This is men's business.'

'Men's business!' Beth scoffed. 'Is that what I'm to tell all the women in this town, when their husbands are shot down and they have to hide their children in

10

some place safe – if there is such a thing? Am I to—?'

'There's nothing more we can discuss right now, gentlemen,' came the judge's calm voice again. 'I think it will be best to close the meeting now and wait for Mr Halliday's arrival.'

There was a shuffle of movement, and almost immediately, the door opened and a streak of light cut across the porch and revealed the horses standing in a sleepy line against the judge's front fence.

Halliday flicked his near-spent cigarette into the yard but remained leaning against the wall. Men filed out, muttering their farewells. Soon the yard was empty. The door was closing when Halliday pushed himself away from the wall and put his hand on the doorknob, holding the door open against the pressure of the person who was closing it from the lamp lit hallway.

Then Halliday was looking down into the questioning brown eyes of a young woman whose beauty immediately made him draw in his breath.

'Yes?'

She let her eyes travel over his clean but wrinkled clothing, the width of his shoulders, and his lean waist before settling finally on the six-gun in the well-worn cutaway holster.

Halliday saw the curiosity in her eyes and then the shocked awareness.

'I'm Halliday,' he said unnecessarily.

Her lips parted but she did not speak or move.

11

She was holding onto the door as if her slender body might be enough to stop him from entering the house.

'Halliday?' came a quick call from inside, and then someone was gently pushing the young woman aside and Halliday was staring straight into the eyes of an old man – tired eyes that still held a gleam of shrewdness and lively interest.

'I'm Judge Cowper. We've been expecting you. Come in, come in, Mr Halliday.'

The girl moved aside and frowned as Halliday entered.

He stepped into the hallway and allowed the judge to close the door behind him.

Cowper moved past him, stopped and looked back at his niece.

'Beth, would you be so kind as to fetch something for Mr Halliday to drink?' A mildly amused smile appeared on his mouth. 'He must be mighty parched after his long ride.'

Beth lifted her chin and gave the judge a look of ladylike defiance. Halliday liked the way she stood with her back so straight and her gaze so direct and honest. Her hair reminded him of corn silk.

'I have no intention of making Mr Halliday welcome in this house, Uncle,' she said in a voice that did not know how to be shrill. 'I ask that you excuse me.'

Cowper frowned and opened his mouth to speak,

but Halliday interrupted him. Hat in hand now, he said quietly;

'That's all right, miss. I understand. I won't be here long anyway, just long enough to get some facts from the judge.'

Beth was surprised by Halliday's quiet voice and mild manner, but the sight of that gun on his hip reminded her of what had been said not long before in the meeting around the judge's dining room table, extended to full size by the addition of the extra leaves.

The talk had run to Halliday's reputation, of course, and someone had remarked that the number of men cut down by that very six-gun was closer to twenty than to ten.

Halliday was a killer-for-hire, and his mere presence revolted her. She moved away without another word, hurrying down the hallway to a room at the other end.

When the door closed behind her, Judge Cowper looked at Halliday and gave a helpless shrug as he pointed the way to the dining room.

'Let's get down to business, Judge,' Halliday said quietly as he pulled out a chair. 'I got your letter, so what is it that needs to be done?'

'I want you to kill a man,' Cowper said, watching for Halliday's reaction.

All he saw was a face devoid of feeling or expression.

13

'What man and for what reason?'

Cowper went across the room to the liquor cabinet and filled two glasses. He brought them to the table and then returned to the cabinet for the bottle, which he placed at Halliday's elbow.

He sat down across the table from his visitor and then immediately launched into his explanation.

'I'm not a violent man, and have never encouraged violence in others. I have lived a life of—'

'I know all about you, Judge,' Halliday interrupted. 'I took the trouble to check you out before I decided to come. You don't have to explain yourself to me. I admire and respect what you've done for this country. I wouldn't be here if I didn't.'

Cowper looked at him with something like gratitude, and took a sip from his glass.

'Thank you, young man. I appreciate you saying that. The reason I called on you is that this town is being wrung dry by one of the most despicable men I have ever had the misfortune to meet. His name is Jason Henley.'

Halliday tasted his drink and listened without interrupting.

'Henley owns the Shimmer Creek Saloon. It is a very good business, and most men would be more than satisfied with it. But not Henley. He is power-hungry and money-hungry, a vicious man who will stop at nothing to get what he wants. In addition, he is now extorting money from the honest merchants

14

of this town in return for protection.'

'Against what?' Halliday asked.

'Himself.'

Halliday frowned, and Cowper gave him a pained smile.

'It is really very simple. Henley approaches people and warns them that the town is becoming violent and they should engage him to protect them. He has a string of very nasty characters on his payroll. . . .'

Halliday finished his drink and helped himself to another. It was good, smooth whiskey, and he was enjoying the way the warmth of it spread slowly through his body.

Cowper leaned forward and spoke with greater urgency now.

'If a person does not pay up, he soon finds out he should have. After a day or so, his place is wrecked and his family threatened. There are plenty of men with gumption in Shimmer Creek – it isn't that we don't want to get our hands dirty, Mr Halliday. It's just that there is no one here who knows how to fight and win against a man like Henley. Some of the men who tried to do that are dead now. Henley's bunch brought others into line by scaring – and mistreating – their womenfolk. This town has lost some very good families, the kind of people a town needs. They just up and left when Shimmer Creek stopped being a peaceful place to raise a family. Everybody that stayed has had no choice but to fall into line.'

'What about the law?' Halliday asked quietly.

Cowper smiled sadly.

'That is where the trouble really lies, Mr Halliday. I've been trying to get somebody to come forward and speak up against Henley, to give me some proof so I can act in a court of law against him. But his men have done their work well – so well, in fact, that I cannot bring myself to criticize or blame anyone who doesn't want to testify. . . .'

'Yeah, Judge,' Halliday said, 'that's understandable, but I guess I was really askin' about law enforcement more than about what goes on in a courthouse.'

'The news is all bad,' Cowper said. 'The sheriff, Rafe Murchison, is on Henley's payroll, too. In fact, I have information that he is Henley's collector. So now you have some idea of what we are up against. Henley is squeezing this town dry. People are sickened by it but helpless to do anything about it. And our lawman is up to his neck in the whole filthy business.'

Cowper wiped a line of sweat from his brow, and contrary to usual habit, he poured himself another drink.

'Beth wouldn't approve of this,' he said wryly as he set the bottle down. 'She fusses over me like a mother hen. . . .'

Halliday settled back in his chair and slowly rolled and lit a cigarette.

'So I'm bein' paid a thousand dollars to take care of Murchison first, and then Henley,' he finally said, rising now and working the tiredness out of his limbs.

'No,' Cowper said urgently. 'Not that far. We don't want a war on our hands. I've been told that you are a match for any man with a gun, Mr Halliday. Rafe Murchison is pretty good with a gun, too. He has proved that point in this town more than once. Henley relies on Murchison – his other hands are just ordinary saloon scum, out for easy money. I've given this a great deal of thought, and I've come to the conclusion that there is only one way to solve our problem.'

A shadow seemed to pass over the old man's face. He looked tired and sad.

'I take Murchison,' said Halliday.

Cowper nodded.

'I've never condoned a thing like this in my life, but what else can we do? With Murchison out of the way, God willing, Henley will give up on what he's doing. Maybe he will sell up and move on, or maybe he will take stock of the situation and decide that the profit he can get from the saloon is enough. Most of the town is behind me in this, and just about every-body has helped raise the money to bring you here. Some people don't agree with me, of course – one of them is my niece, as you've just discovered.' He gave a faint smile and added, 'After all my years on the

17

bench, I have plenty of experience in making decisions that are not always popular. I've thought long and hard on this, and I truly believe this is the best way to get Shimmer Creek back on its feet. Do we understand each other, Mr Halliday?'

Halliday nodded, finished his third drink and set down the empty glass. Cowper went to a desk and brought out a bulging envelope. He handed it over, and there was a hint of relief in his voice when he said, 'One thousand dollars paid in full, Mr Halliday. Naturally, I wish you luck. As for accommodation, I've arranged to put you up at the rooming house on Washington Street, at the town's expense. See Mr Lattimer there. He can be trusted, and he is right behind me in this.'

Cowper moved across the room and opened the door. Halliday went past him, stuffing the envelope in his shirt without bothering to count it.

There was a movement from the far end of the hallway, and Halliday turned his head.

The light was dim, but it almost seemed to Beth that the gunman smiled at her for just a moment.

Then he was gone, and soon afterward, the sound of his horse's hoof beats drifted back to the two people standing close together in the doorway.

'It is the only way, girl,' Cowper said wearily. 'God knows I looked for another solution, but there is none. There is just no other way to fight scum like Henley and Murchison. I am quite sure that I have found the right man for the job, Beth.'

The young woman touched her uncle lightly on the arm.

'Go to bed now, Uncle. You've had a trying time and nothing more can be done now.'

Buck Halliday left his horse in the rooming house yard and returned by way of the back street to the saloon. He had never been in this part of the country before. It was likely that most folks would know his name, but he doubted that any of the locals would recognize him on sight. Though it was always possible that some drifter had crossed his trail in another town, of course.

He entered the saloon by the back door and bought a bottle of whiskey. He melted into the crowd as best he could, surveying the other customers before he ducked out the back door again.

He was standing in the yard and checking it out in his usual careful manner when he heard a stifled cry from the darkness opposite. Looking that way, he saw the outline of a shack with two figures standing close together on the tiny porch.

'You're just a pig of a man, Jason, nothin' but a goddamn pig,' a woman said in a high, angry voice.

The next thing Halliday heard was a sharp slap, followed by a groan. The woman stumbled off the porch and fetched up against the hitching rail.

Halliday saw her bend down suddenly and come

up with what looked like a barrel stave in her hand.

The man who had hit her was down the steps and reaching for her as she swung the stave and hit him across the face with such force that her makeshift weapon broke into pieces.

The man spat blood and cursed but held his ground. Halliday saw him shake his head in an apparent effort to clear it and then reach for the woman again. He caught her by the shoulder, and Halliday heard the fabric tear as the bodice of her dress came away in his hand.

The woman dragged one arm free and came back with an openhanded slap that echoed in the quiet of the yard.

'That's enough, you silly little bitch,' the man said thickly, and Halliday saw his hand make a fist.

It was a hard punch, and the woman fell to the ground and stayed there.

Halliday carefully set down his bottle, and then he moved in fast, catching the man's arm and swinging him around so that he could sink his fist hard into the man's belly. As the man folded forward, Halliday came up with an uppercut that landed right on the point of the man's jaw.

The man staggered a step or two and then collapsed. The woman was up and running toward the saloon with her torn dress fluttering behind her. Halliday picked up his bottle and turned to go. He was annoyed at himself for getting involved in an argument that was none of his business, but he purely hated to see a big man beating up on a little woman.

He was halfway to the back corner of the saloon where he had last seen the woman when a voice growled, 'You there, hold on!'

Halliday turned and transferred the bottle to his left hand. In the light from the saloon, he saw the silhouette of a bowlegged man with his hand resting on his gun butt.

The man was shocked into silence by the speed of Halliday's draw.

'Mind your own damn business!' Halliday told him.

'Yeah, yeah,' the man nodded in a sudden change of heart. 'Got nothin' to do with me, I guess.'

With his eyes fixed on Halliday's gun hand, he backed up until he felt the bottom step with his heel. Then he whirled and rushed into the saloon.

Halliday went back to the man in the yard, who was out cold. He glanced down at the bloodied face so that he would remember it if he saw it again, and then he headed back to Lattimer's rooming house.

A quiet drink or two and a soft bed had a lot more to offer than a dust-up in the dark with a bunch of saloon drunks.

TWO

JULIE

The man at the desk was bald and short, and his face twitched nervously as wide-spaced eyes lifted anxiously to watch Buck Halliday cross the foyer. He could see by the gunrig and the nonchalant confidence that this was no drummer with a suitcase full of combs and sewing notions.

Halliday went straight to the desk, and without invitation, he spun the ledger around and reached for a pen.

'Halliday,' he said. 'I think you're holdin' a room for me.'

The man sucked in a quick breath and tried for a smile.

'Yes, Mr Halliday, I am. My name's Walsh Lattimer, and you're mighty welcome here. No need to sign, you're in the book. You have Room 7, upstairs at the back. It's as separate from the other boarders as I can manage.'

'Obliged,' Halliday told him, and picked up the key which the man produced from a board under his desk.

Then the man leaned forward, expecting to see a warbag at Halliday's feet.

'Travelin' light, eh, Mr Halliday?' Lattimer asked in a knowing tone.

'I left my horse and my belongin's in the stall out back,' Halliday said. 'No sense in unpackin' tonight.'

'No sense a-tall, Mr Halliday. Anything you want now, just ask.'

'I'd like some supper,' Halliday told him, and then his attention shifted to the woman who had just slipped in by a side door. She had one hand clapped to her torn dress, holding it in place to cover herself.

'Why, Mrs Henley,' exclaimed the desk man. 'What are you doing? What's happened to you?'

Without answering, the woman walked up to Halliday and introduced herself.

'I'm Julie Henley. You're the man who helped me just awhile ago, aren't you?'

'I thought he was goin' to kill you,' Halliday said simply.

'I expect he would have, if it wasn't for you,' she said. 'Are you stayin' here, mister?'

'Yes.'

The woman looked at the man behind the desk, and said quickly, 'I'm in some trouble, Mr Lattimer. I need time to sort myself out. Do you mind if I stay here for an hour or so?'

Lattimer could not take his eyes off the soft, pink flesh that showed through the torn dress, but he managed to nod and mumble, 'No, Mrs Henley, I don't mind a-tall. There ain't goin' to be no trouble, is there?'

'Not unless you tell him I'm here.'

Lattimer shook his head and looked around. When he saw that the woman had left the side door open, he hurried to close it before scurrying back to his desk.

The woman turned back to Halliday, looking him up and down in serious appraisal. Then she posed her question bluntly;

'Would you mind, Mr. . . ?'

'Would I mind what, Mrs Henley?'

'If I depended on your protection for another hour. I do need time to think. That man you saw hittin' me was my husband and, after what I did to him, he'll want to tear the town apart to find me. If he does, I don't like to think what might happen to me.'

Halliday scratched the back of his neck absently, and then he shrugged. The woman interested him, by name anyway. To Lattimer, he said;

'Might as well keep this quiet. Room seven, huh?'

'End of the corridor up the stairs,' Lattimer nodded.

'Come on then,' Halliday said to the woman as he started toward the stairway.

He saw the quick uplift of her brows, and then she followed him to the stairs.

'Don't forget that supper,' Halliday called down to Lattimer from halfway up the stairs.

He found the room at the end of a narrow corridor, with access to a balcony that wrapped around the end of the two-storied building.

When he opened the door, the woman slipped past him, brushing her body lightly against his chest.

He saw immediate interest in her eyes and a smile touched her soft, full lips.

Halliday closed the door and watched while she poured water into a basin and dabbed blood from her lips and neck. She inspected her bruised features in the mirror above the washstand and made a rueful face at what she saw. Then she turned and looked at Halliday in a way that needed no explanation.

Halliday paced the room, looking out the window and even pulling back the curtain that covered a corner where clothes hooks were mounted on the wall.

The woman seated herself on the edge of the bed and watched him with unwavering interest.

He moved the easy chair to a spot facing the bed

and flopped into it.

'Who are you?' Julie Henley asked.

'Doesn't matter who I am, Mrs Henley.'

'My name is Julie. Please call me that. I get sick in the stomach every time somebody calls me Mrs Henley. I'd rather be known as kin to a rattlesnake.'

Halliday smiled at that but retained a good degree of caution.

The woman leaned back against the bed head and lifted her hands above her head to tidy her hair. The torn bodice of her dress dropped down, exposing creamy lace and a half-moon of soft, white skin. She looked down at the torn garment and it seemed to offend her. She took the loose fabric in her hands and tore it away from the dress, all the way to her narrow waist. Smiling at him, she dropped the torn piece to the floor beside her.

'I'm afraid this dress is good for nothin' more than dust rags now,' she pouted. 'And you're right, mister. It doesn't matter who you are. All I need to know about you is that you are the only man I've met in years who has what it takes to put my husband in his place. I want you, Mr Whoever-you-are, and it isn't just because I'm feelin' grateful.'

Halliday uncorked his whiskey bottle and drank from the neck. Then he wiped the neck with his hand and held the bottle out to her.

Julie slipped off the bed and walked slowly to his chair. She took the bottle and tipped it back for a taste and then a swallow.

Then she bent over him to place the bottle beside his chair. She reached for his hand and rubbed it against her thigh. He could feel the warmth of her skin through the gauzy summer fabric.

Halliday continued to look at her, but his gaze was so dispassionate that he might have been guessing the weight of a steer.

When she released his hand, it dropped to his side.

Julie's eyes fired with mild disappointment, but then she reached behind her back and slowly undid the hooks and eyes that held the remnants of her dress in place. The garment fell around her feet.

She looked up at Halliday and saw no change in his expression. He was taking another pull on the bottle but still watching her as he swallowed.

She pulled at the bow on a satin ribbon, and her petticoat joined the dress with a whisper of lace and ruffles.

Although he was not ready to let her see it, Halliday could feel desire building inside him.

His mind was still dealing with the facts and questions of what she was, who she was, and why she was here. He thought she was telling the truth when she said it did not matter who he was. She was playing this game to its limit to spite her husband. Maybe that did not matter either. The feelings that were beginning to steam the windows in this pokey little rented room had nothing to do with hearts and flowers and a romantic need to know the loved one's middle name and family history.

Julie stepped out of her clothes and stood there, a goddessed package of everything woman-starved men of the frontier craved. Halliday placed the bottle on the dresser table then removed his gunbelt and flung it across the dresser mirror. She came to him and ran her fingers through his hair and brought his head against her soft warm body. His hands stole to her back and he felt her giving with the hesitant pressure he applied.

She was beginning to purr like a cat already.

And then he stopped.

Julie stiffened and saw that he seemed to be listening for something in the corridor outside his room.

'It's all right,' she said urgently. 'Neither of us has anything to worry about . . . for the moment.'

Halliday eased her back, took one step to the dresser and pulled his gun from the holster.

Julie frowned in frustration, but then she heard it, too – a tiny sound outside the door and then the light scratch of a key in the lock. The door began to open slowly, and Julie snatched up her dress and held it in front of her.

The first thing they saw in the crack of the opening door was the barrel of a gun, then the entire gun and the hand of the man who was holding it.

Halliday was across the room in an instant, kicking the door hard against the extended hand. When the hand jerked back, Halliday pulled the door wide open, grabbed the intruder by the shoulder and dragged him into the room.

He slammed his fist into the stranger's face and kicked the man's legs out from under him. The man hit the corner of the dresser as he fell, and Julie jumped back with a little squeak as the man struggled to rise.

Reversing the six-gun in his hand, Halliday thumped the butt against the side of the man's head.

This time, the man fell so hard the whiskey bottle and the washbasin danced and rattled. He was still trying to get to his feet, but his eyes had gone blank and he pitched forward, hitting the bunk and sliding to the floor.

When the man did not move again, Halliday turned him onto his back with the toe of his boot. That was the first time he noticed the tarnished tin star.

Halliday gave Julie Henley a questioning look, and she whispered;

'It's our sheriff, Rafe Murchison.'

Without comment, Halliday returned his six-gun to the holster and tucked in his shirttail. With his eyes on the unconscious lawman, he reached for the bottle on the dresser, pulling the stopper with his teeth and taking a long swallow. Finally, Julie said;

'He's a friend of my husband's. He'll tell him everything.'

She dropped the dress again and reached up to tidy her hair.

'Put your clothes on,' Halliday said coldly, 'and get the hell outta here. Ma'am, you're a complication I can do without!'

Julie glared at him and hissed, 'You're not afraid of him, are you? Why, he's just a hired hand, and not a very good one at that. He might be all right with a gun, or so they say, but I've never seen him tackle anyone on his own – not even a harmless old drunk. Anyway, we can go someplace else. . . .'

'You can go someplace else, Mrs Henley,' Halliday said wearily. 'Now good night.'

On the floor, Murchison was groaning as he slowly regained consciousness.

Halliday lifted him by the front of his shirt and hauled him onto the bed. He kicked Murchison's gun under the bed and picked up the basin of water that was already tinted with Julie's blood. He pushed the lawman's face into the water until the man began to choke and cough, and then he returned the basin to the washstand.

The sheriff's eyes were in focus now, and his lips peeled back in a snarl.

'You're gonna regret doin' that, mister—'

'Take it easy, Murchison, and answer a few questions. For one, how did you find out my room number?'

'That's my business.'

Halliday looked in Julie's direction. She had stepped behind the curtain and was hurriedly pulling on her clothes.

'Did you tell him?' Halliday asked her.

Julie scowled. 'Me? What are you talkin' about?'

'Strange how you just happened on the scene at the right moment, Mrs Henley. Are you and Murchison in cahoots, by any chance. . . ?'

'Listen, you poor excuse for a man!' Julie snapped. 'Who do you think you are anyway? As far as I'm concerned, you and Murchison and everybody else in this flea-bitten town can go to hell – and the sooner the better!'

Both Halliday and Murchison watched the woman struggle into her torn and crumpled clothes. From the waist up, the dress was hardly big enough, and the lacy contraption under it seemed designed to display more than it concealed. Deciding that she had made the best of it, Julie folded her arms over her bosom and pushed past Halliday on her way to the door.

'I can see you think you're somethin' pretty special, Halliday,' the sheriff said from the bed, 'but you could get yourself tarred and feathered, maybe lynched for dishonorin' another man's wife like you

31

done. Besides, you resisted arrest and beat up on one of the most important men in this town. Iffen I was you, I'd get the hell outta here while you got the chance. . . .'

'Henley asked for what he got,' was Halliday's simple response, and he picked up the whiskey bottle and carried it to the doorway.

He could hear Julie running down the stairs, no doubt hunting for another place to hide. He felt somewhat sorry for the wayward young woman, but he guessed that she was the kind who always found trouble or made some of her own.

'I'm warning you, Halliday,' the sheriff insisted, 'get out of town while you got the chance, or you'll go out feet first.'

'Thanks for the warnin',' Halliday said calmly, 'and now I have one for you. I'm gonna get you, but not right now. It's gonna be in front of plenty of witnesses. So I'm givin' you a choice, if you can savvy that. You can run or you can suffer the consequences.'

'You think you're that good?' Murchison asked softly.

'I know I am. If you stick around until tomorrow, sunup, you'll know it, too. So get off my bed and get outta my room!'

Rubbing his rapidly swelling jaw, Murchison got off the bed and went out the door without further comment. He would be the first to admit that

Halliday packed quite a punch, but in his mind, gunplay was something else.

Halliday followed the man to the back stairs. Murchison stopped and looked back before he started down.

'I'm givin' you fair warnin', Halliday, and no hard feelin's,' the lawman said. 'You can't win this one. It's too big for you or anybody else. The part about the girl doesn't matter. You aren't the first, and Henley knows it. She's a tramp.'

The words and even the tone of voice were perfectly reasonable, but the knowing smirk on the lawman's face gave out another message.

Halliday's fist snaked out with such speed that Murchison could do nothing to protect himself. The blow knocked him off his feet and he slid and bumped all the way to the bottom. He landed head-first with a thud that made the whole stairway shudder.

Halliday saw him try to stand, but he pitched forward into the darkness instead.

'Okay,' Halliday muttered, 'we've all had our warnin's.'

Halliday turned his back on the battered lawman and went down the hallway in search of Lattimer and the long-delayed supper.

There was no one at the desk or in the dining room, so Halliday followed his nose to the kitchen.

The coffeepot was close to boiling dry. On the

33

warming shelf above the hotplates, a large steak was congealing in its own juices. Halliday plucked the steak from the plate and began to eat it from his hand as he sauntered back into the dining room. The table had been laid for breakfast, and the cloth concealed what lay beneath it, except for one foot.

Still chewing on the steak, Halliday squatted down and lifted the edge of the tablecloth.

'Well,' he said, 'I see it ain't your fault my supper's gone cold.'

Lattimer's head lay at an unnatural angle to his body, and his round eyes stared at Halliday with the blankness of death.

Halliday dragged the corpse out from under the table and contemplated the marks on the face, neck and arms.

At least he knew now that Julie Henley had not led him into a trap, and that Lattimer had tried his best to protect him.

Halliday took another bite of steak and returned to the kitchen, where he returned the bone to the plate and took a long drink of water from the pump at the sink.

Then he remembered the man who had called to him behind the saloon. That could well be the man behind all this.

Halliday wiped his hands carefully on the kitchen towel and headed out to the yard.

Murchison was no longer in sight.

Cussing in frustration, Halliday went to check on his horse. He saw that someone, no doubt Walsh Lattimer, had fed and watered the sorrel without being asked.

He returned to the boardinghouse by the back door and locked the door behind him. He found that the front door already had been locked for the night.

Resignedly, Halliday returned to the kitchen and started a fresh pot of coffee. He would stay there to wait out the night.

Judge Cowper awoke to a loud hammering on his back door. He was still searching groggily for his robe and slippers when he heard Beth say, 'Well, what do you want now, Mr Halliday?'

'I have to see the judge. Something's come up he should know about.'

'You've done your killing already and think you deserve a bonus, is that it?' Beth asked coldly.

'Just get your uncle, ma'am. I haven't time for small talk.'

Beth stiffened and put her hand on the door as if she meant to slam it in Halliday's face. Then her uncle was behind her.

'What is it, Mr Halliday?' Cowper asked anxiously.

'Lattimer's dead,' Halliday told him bluntly.

'How did it happen?' Cowper asked heavily.

'Somebody broke his neck. I think Murchison did it.'

Cowper rocked backward as if Halliday had struck him in the face.

'Are you sure? You know, if we can prove he did it, we won't have to go through with the other idea—'

'There's no proof that will stand up in a court of law, Judge,' Halliday told him. 'Just take it from me, he did it. Looks to me like the sooner this business is over and done, the better. What I want from you is some rope and then, in say fifteen minutes, I want some of your friends linin' the main street.'

Beth moved back into the kitchen and absently began to stuff the fire door on the stove with fresh kindling.

'Rope, you say,' Cowper muttered.

He went into the backyard and returned with a coil of rope. As he handed it over, he said;

'There's about thirty feet there. What do you intend to do with it?'

'What you paid me to do, Judge,' Halliday said. 'I'm tryin' to keep this between Murchison and me instead of turnin' it into a shootin' war with every man on Henley's payroll. Remember, Judge, I want folks out on the street in fifteen minutes.'

Beth watched him from the window, unnerved by his calm and confused in her feelings. Halliday was certainly a killer, but maybe the judge was right . . . only a killer could save their town.

Buck Halliday carefully checked out the back of the

saloon in the dim light of morning. There was no sound to indicate that anyone was stirring in the saloon or in the living quarters behind it. A lamp was still burning somewhere toward the front of the building. Maybe it always did.

Halliday went quietly up the back steps and let himself in. When he looked down from the landing, he saw seven men sitting at the card tables, most of them bowed over in sleep. One man sat alone at the bar, staring at the label on the bottle in front of him as though it carried an important message.

Halliday drew his gun and moved a step or two to the right, so that he had a clear line of fire.

'Henley, if you move, you're a dead man!'

The man at the bar turned quickly, and Halliday knew that he had guessed right. Henley's mouth was swollen and his right shoulder dipped lower than his left as the result of an injury.

The big man's right hand had dropped to his gun butt, but he made no attempt to take it further.

'Halliday?' Henley asked.

'That's right, mister.'

Some of the men were stirring at the tables now, and Halliday raised his voice so that everyone could hear him.

'If anybody makes a move, your boss is gonna be the first one to get it. Maybe you don't like him much, but just remember, when he dies, you'll be out of a job.'

A bead of sweat showed on Henley's brow, and he asked;

'What do you want, Halliday? What've I done to you?'

'Just shuck that gunrig and get over here quick!' Halliday snapped. 'If you really want to know, you haven't done a thing to me. It's what you're doin' to this town – and what you did to your wife last night – that's bringin' all this trouble down on you. In other words, mister, you only have yourself to blame.'

Henley wiped his clammy hands on his pants and unbuckled the gunrig. It hit the floor with a dull thump, and then he started slowly across the room.

Halliday gestured toward the back of the saloon, and said, 'Keep goin'. I'll be behind you all the way.' He looked back at the men around the card tables then, and said, 'If you boys have the brains God gave you, you'll stay where you are and keep your hands away from your guns.'

As he followed Henley into the yard, he heard a buzz of voices and the scrape of chair legs behind him.

'This way,' he said to Henley after checking out the alley on their way to the main street.

'Wait a minute,' he told the saloon man while he looked out onto the widest street in town. 'Okay. Across the street.'

Right on schedule, Judge Cowper and Beth were walking toward them from the business block, accompanied by a group of grim-faced townsmen.

A block or so behind them, Julie Henley was stepping out of the bank building, on the arm of a distinguished-looking man twice her age.

'Over here,' Halliday said as he prodded Henley toward an awning post. 'Now hold still.'

'What the hell do you think you're doing?' Henley snarled.

'Can't you tell?' Halliday replied. 'I'm tyin' you up like a hog for slaughter.'

'How much are they paying you?'

'Enough,' Halliday told him, and took another hard pull on the ropes to test them. 'Now you just stay right here like a good boy, huh?'

With Henley's curses fouling the air behind him, Halliday checked his six-gun and proceeded slowly along the boardwalk until he was across the street from the jailhouse.

He fired once at the front window.

Almost immediately, Henley's hired hands came rushing out of the saloon and the front door of the jailhouse flew open.

Not surprisingly, the sheriff did not show himself.

Halliday faded back along the boardwalk until he was standing behind Henley.

'Murchison,' he announced, 'I'm callin' you for the murder of Walsh Lattimer.'

Murchison remained in the dimness of his doorway for a long minute. Then he squared his shoulders and stepped out into the light.

'You don't scare me, Halliday,' he said.

'That's good. It will save us both some time. So let's quit wastin' words and get it over with. . . .'

'How damn much, Halliday?' Henley barked. 'I'll double whatever they're payin' you. Murchison ain't no slouch, so why take chances for no good reason?'

'I saw what this sheriff of yours did to Walsh Lattimer – for no good reason. You best shut your trap before I decide you gave him the orders.'

Henley's face drained of color and he struggled to free himself, but Halliday had hitched too many horses and roped too many steers to tie a knot that would come loose when it was meant to hold.

Rafe Murchison's eyes slid to the boardwalks and saw that they were beginning to fill with people who were tired of living without law. He settled his gunbelt a little lower on his waist and stepped into the street to begin his slow, short walk to destiny.

There was no wind and no sound at all but the steady, determined footsteps of a lawman who had bloodied his hands and tarnished his badge.

THREE

BULLET FOR A LAWMAN

'Hold it there, Halliday!'

This new voice drifted out of the saloon, and its owner shouldered his way through the crowd at the door.

He was a big, bony man of about forty, with a six-gun steady as a rock in his fist. He looked and sounded every inch the gunfighter.

Rafe Murchison stopped dead in his tracks, flexing his fingers as his hands hung loose at his sides.

'I figure this has gone far enough,' the man from the saloon said flatly. 'Let Henley loose right now. You can ride out of this in one piece, and nobody will care.'

'Figure what you like, mister,' Buck Halliday said. 'I've been paid to do a job, just like you, from the look of it. If that's how you want it, I'll just have to drop you, too – right after Murchison and Henley.'

'Dammit, Sharpe!' Jason Henley snapped. 'Nobody asked you to horn in on this. Rafe'll take him, you'll see.'

The gunman shook his head slowly.

'No, boss,' Sharpe said. 'Rafe can't handle him. I seen this feller once in Abilene. He don't ever lose.'

Murchison hesitated and glared at the man called Sharpe, showing the blunt courage of someone who depended on reputation to make his way in life.

'Mister,' Halliday said to Sharpe, 'I don't know about you, but I don't have such a taste for killin' that I do more than I have to. Even your boss seems to think there's no reason for us to tangle, and I reckon he's right. I came here for Murchison and nobody else. After that, I'll be on my way.'

Sharpe looked toward Henley a moment longer, his brow furrowed in thought.

'We can get him, boss,' he said. 'He's just one man against all of us.'

'And have me killed, you damn fool? I pay Rafe to protect me, and it looks to me like he's willing to do his job. Now you just shut your fool mouth and stay outta this.'

'Sharpe, if you try anything, we will shoot you down where you stand,' Judge Cowper suddenly called from the boardwalk.

Sharpe whirled and found himself looking straight into the yawning barrels of the old judge's scattergun.

The expression on the old man's face told Sharpe that Cowper meant what he said.

Sharpe cursed sourly and glared at his companions, but no one would meet his eyes.

Beth tried to step up beside her uncle, but the old man shook his head and said;

'Stay behind me, girl.'

Murchison had begun to move forward again, but try as he might, he could not get Sharpe's words out of his mind:

'Rafe can't handle him . . . he don't ever lose.'

Halliday glanced at the sweating man tied to the post beside him.

'Well, Henley? Looks like you're callin' the shots, so what's it gonna be – a gunfight between me and Murchison, or a turkey shoot with you caught in the crossfire?'

'Everybody stay outta this!' Henley yelled. 'I mean it!'

Halliday nodded and returned to the street to face the advancing sheriff.

Murchison stopped again and flexed his gun hand. Now his unwavering stare was fixed on Halliday.

A deep silence settled on the street. No one

moved or even seemed to breathe. Halliday's voice was soft when he said, 'All Walsh Lattimer did was run a boardinghouse, Murchison. From the little I saw, he didn't look like he could bring himself to hurt a fly. And you beat him to death. For that, you deserve to die.'

Murchison licked his lips and rolled his shoulders.

'Dammit,' he snarled suddenly, 'this ain't no talkin' match!' His hand plunged down to his holster and his fingers curled in place around the butt and the trigger as the gun swept into line.

Cowper watched Halliday and was shocked to see him wait until the moment Murchison's gun cleared leather.

Then Halliday's hand blurred, a gunshot cut the silence, and Murchison rocked back on his heels.

The impact of the bullet in his chest splayed the sheriff's fingers wide, and although he clenched them again in an effort to fire, he never touched the trigger. His legs buckled and he fell forward on his face.

Halliday's eyes were on Sharpe now, and he saw the gunman's right hand twitch.

'That's it,' Halliday said with finality. 'We're all through, folks. Get that mess off the street and bury it. Unless the rest of you hired hands think you can take up where Murchison left off, it looks to me like this town is free again – and it's up to the decent folks to find an honest man and keep it that way.'

Halliday backed around Henley and gave an

expert pull at the ropes. Then he pushed the man away from the post.

'I think you better do some hard thinkin' now, mister,' Halliday said. 'You could be the one lyin' out there in the street.'

Henley seemed to be too shocked to speak, but he nodded dumbly and shambled toward the saloon, rubbing at his numbed wrists.

Everyone else stood their ground until the judge nodded and turned to take Beth home.

When Henley reached the boardwalk outside his saloon, he broke into a run and dived through the batwings.

'Get him, Bob!' Henley yelled from the safety of the saloon. 'Get 'em all!'

Halliday was ready. He leveled his gun on Bob Sharpe and waited for the man to draw. Sharpe's bullet went wide of its mark, and thudded into the plank siding of an attorney's office.

Almost casually, Halliday carefully placed his shot.

The bunch that had been backing Sharpe faded into the saloon like smoke in a high wind.

Meantime, Henley had taken a gun from under the counter and was yelling at his men to take up positions at the windows. Halliday knew what was coming, and he was taking cover on the other side of the street.

Henley opened fire, but Halliday sent him scurrying a moment later with a well-placed bullet.

'Lee!' Henley yelled to one of his men. 'Knock out that front window so you can get a clear shot at the bastard!'

Obligingly, Lee Mitchener averted his face and smashed the window with his gun butt. Then he laid a volley of gunfire across the street where Halliday was sheltering until his gun hammer clicked on empty.

Halliday immediately retaliated, and one of his bullets skimmed Mitchener's temple, knocking him senseless.

In the lull that followed, Halliday simply walked under the shadow of the awnings until he came to an alley that took him into a quiet back street.

Judge Cowper slumped into his porch rocker and put his head in his hands so that he was staring blankly between his fingers at the unpainted floor-boards between his feet.

'You can't blame yourself, Uncle,' Beth said quietly. 'Everybody was behind you. Everybody agreed that hiring Mr Halliday was the sensible thing to do.'

Cowper shook his head miserably but did not look up.

'Four men dead,' he said. 'I didn't want it to come to that. Halliday let me down. He said he'd—'

'They shot at him, Uncle,' Beth reasoned. 'We couldn't expect him just to stand there and be killed.'

Cowper raked his fingers through his hair and rubbed the back of his neck.

Slowly, he nodded, and then he got shakily to his feet and went to the porch rail. Leaning heavily on the railing, he looked out over the town in which not a single man, horse or dog moved.

'He knew what they would do, girl. He egged them on. He knew what Sharpe and Henley were like from the start, and he made no effort to stop things before they went too far.'

'Well, it's over now, Uncle. There's no point in crying over what's done, is there? Mr Halliday did what you paid him to do, and, in fact, he did more. Jason Henley will rue the day he ever laid eyes on Buck Halliday.'

'He'll rue it all right, girl!' Cowper snapped. 'And he'll do his damndest to get even. Henley showed some grit today. I didn't think he had it in him, and I'm sure Halliday didn't think it, either. We both underestimated him. Henley is going to try to pay us all back for what Halliday did to him, and how on earth can we stop him?'

'Mr Halliday has not left yet, Uncle,' Beth reminded him. 'A good part of this added trouble is his fault, so why don't you ask him to fix it?'

Cowper gave his gentle niece a look of concern. As much as anything, he regretted exposing her to the violence which had scarred their town so terribly. He reached out and pulled her to him, then said firmly;

'Keep out of it, Beth. This has been too much for you already. I will see Halliday and talk to him. He might be able to advise us on what to do. But I'll pay him no more money – you can be sure of that.'

Beth kissed him lightly on the cheek and drew away, leaving him to make his way down the path to the street. Before the old man could open the gate, Halliday came riding down the street in full view.

Beth stopped in the doorway and watched him fixedly. When he reined-in at the gate, she found that she could not bring herself to turn away.

She was fascinated by his self-assurance. He looked for all the world like an ordinary man going about everyday business of the dullest kind.

Halliday stayed in the saddle and turned his horse so that he was watching the street behind him as he spoke to the judge.

'I know that wasn't what you wanted, Judge,' he said blandly. 'I'm sorry it turned out like it did.'

'That is quite an understatement, Mr Halliday,' the old man said stiffly. 'I was hoping that by making a show of strength and ridding the town of Rafe Murchison, we could convince Jason Henley to behave decently. I fear your actions have had the opposite effect.'

Halliday regarded the judge steadily, and then he said, 'So what now?'

'You will have to tell me that, Mr Halliday. You went too far. You killed four of his men—'

'Four less for you to worry about, Judge,' Halliday was quick to remind him.

Cowper gripped the gate post so hard his knuckles turned white.

'I did not want a bloodbath, Mr Halliday. I've made a damn old fool of myself by bringing you here. I should have known better.'

'We all make mistakes,' Halliday said sympathetically, but Cowper would not be put off.

'You are my mistake, Mr Halliday, and heaven knows that I will be glad to see the back of you.'

Halliday frowned slightly.

'Don't overdo it, Judge,' he cautioned. 'The best thing you can do now is get yourself some men you can trust and ram home the advantage. Henley's pulled back to lick his wounds, but it won't be long before he breaks out again. Men like Murchison can be easily replaced, and if you wait too long, Henley will be ready for you next time.'

'Henley can go to hell! At least I've managed to give the town a little backbone. I saw quite a few of my friends willing to fight today. Who knows? They might discover that their new-found courage might be permanent.'

Halliday shrugged and patted the sorrel's neck. The horse seemed to be absorbing the rider's desire to be gone.

'You want me to go, Judge?'

'Right away. As long as you stay, there will be

trouble in this town. Henley won't rest until he cuts you down. That's the last thing we need – it will make him more arrogant than ever.'

'Yeah,' Halliday said softly. 'It's nice to know you've got one reason to be glad I'm still alive.'

Beth came hurrying down the path. She had been unable to hear much of the conversation, but she could see that her uncle was fast losing his temper.

She was surprised to see that Halliday merely tipped his hat to her and put his horse into a walk. He was a hundred yards away and heading out of town when a bunch of riders charged out of a cross street and headed straight for him.

Beth gasped and tried to pull her uncle back toward the house, but Cowper shrugged off her grip.

'Halliday, watch out!' Cowper yelled. 'To your right!'

The call was not necessary. Halliday had heard the horses coming, and perhaps he had sensed them before that. He drew his gun and galloped his horse into the yards at the very end of the street. Dropping from the saddle, he took cover and trained his sights on the horsemen. There were four of them, including a man with a bandage around his head.

The color drained from Beth's face. She expected to see Halliday cut to shreds, but she could not bring herself to look away. Then her uncle rasped;

'That man has guts. I have to give him that. . . .'

Beth watched Halliday drop to the ground and go

into a roll as another volley of gunfire rattled the rails of the corral.

Then one of the riders jumped his horse over the top rail, skidded to a dust-churning halt, and came charging back at Halliday from behind. The horseman got so close to Halliday that it seemed to Beth he would be trampled, but then Halliday fired and Beth saw the horseman lurch in the saddle and clutch at his throat.

Cowper came back to her and guided her along the path to the house, both of them still watching the gunfight in awe.

Halliday ducked as another horse leaped the corral fence. For one split-second, he was caught in the crossfire of two men outside the yard and one inside, but then he was standing his ground and firing so quickly that the gunshots became a continuous roar.

The two men outside the corral heeled their mounts out of range, but the rider who had jumped the fence was bearing down on him. His six-gun was empty, but he coolly slipped a bullet into the chamber and stood his ground.

It took only seconds, but it was a battle of nerves, and Lee Mitchener was the loser. He wrenched on the reins and swung his horse wide of the man with a gun who was grinning up at him. Mitchener spurred and crouched low in the saddle, taking the horse over the rails and racing to join his companions. There was a crawling sensation between his shoulder blades, as everything in him waited for the bullet that did not come.

It was too much for Beth to bear. She took the steps at a run and kept going until she collapsed in a chair deep within the house. The judge slowly followed her. Now more than ever, he looked a tired old man.

He turned back on the top step and saw Buck Halliday climbing into the saddle. He did not seem to be hurrying, and there was no sign that he had been hurt.

Without a backward glance, Halliday rode out of town.

FOUR

HENLEY'S HENCHMEN

Jason Henley picked up a bottle and hurled it angrily across the room. When it hit the wall, glass and whiskey sprayed back over the empty card tables and the motionless roulette wheel. There was no one who could tell him to stop. The saloon and the whiskey and the four men were all his.

'Are you real proud of yourselves?' Henley snarled. 'Well, you oughta be. Nine against one, and he gave you the lickin' of your lives. The whole damn town is laughin' about it, you know. Laughin' at me!'

When Henley stopped for breath, there was no other sound to fill the silence. His last four men

53

looked anywhere but in his direction, and no one had a word to say.

Ben Albert had been with him for only two months. Mitchener had a serious head wound, and now it was throbbing like a big bass drum. Bassett was too old and slow now to get out of his own way. Luke Shelton was wild enough to try anything, but he was also young and green.

Lee Mitchener walked behind the counter and brought out a fresh bottle, but Henley grabbed it out of his hand and that just meant that more spilled whiskey and flying glass hit the wall.

'No free drinks for you!' Henley snapped with all the conviction of a teetotaler. 'Nobody touches a goddamn drop until we get this town back where I want it. That damn Cowper is sittin' at home right now, laughin' himself into a fit at the way Halliday treated us. Just one man, and he whipped nine of you and walked away without so much as a goddamn scratch. One against nine! I might as well have hired the church choir. Come to think of it, I might have been better off that way. Some of them ladies look like they could beat hell out of any man. They wouldn't even need a gun – just a hatpin and a hymn book. . . .'

'Halliday ain't just any man,' Mitchener muttered resentfully.

'Is that so?' Henley snarled. 'Maybe you want to tell me what's so different about him. Looked to me like he had two arms and two legs and one gun, just like all nine of you. That's all it took to beat you today. And you know what that means? We didn't just lose everything we gained in the last six months. No, sir. Now we're further behind than when we started. Who the hell is gonna pay good money to keep themselves safe from an outfit one man can lick without even raisin' a sweat? Anybody like to tell me the answer to that? How about you, Lee? Want to take a guess at how much money you're likely to collect now, if I send you out on the street with that bandage wrapped around your head and that hangdog look on your face?'

Mitchener scowled blackly back at him.

'Dammit, boss,' he cussed. 'We did what we could, and you know it. I'm tellin' you straight, I'm just grateful that he's gone. I want no part of him.'

Tom Basset grunted agreement, Ben Albert nodded. Only Luke Shelton looked like he still had some fight left in him.

Henley glared at his hired guns for almost a minute, and then he snorted in disgust and began to pace up and down the barroom, his feet crunching on broken glass every time he reached the far end of the room.

When he finally stopped, it appeared that he had come to a decision.

'All right, what's done is done, but so help me, things are gonna tighten up around here, startin' right now. First we got to put Cowper in his place. That's the best way to keep the rest of this town under our thumb. I'm gettin' a replacement for Rafe, but until he gets here, we'll just have to play it quiet. Nobody makes trouble, nobody gets drunk, nobody walks the streets on his own. Better still, nobody walks the streets at all unless I say so. You can get everything you want in here. It's gonna be business as usual, and we're gonna make it look like we've all decided to behave ourselves and just run the saloon. Hear me?'

When the men nodded back at him, Henley wiped his sweating face on a handkerchief and walked to the swing doors.

When he saw the bullet holes in the timber, he was reminded again of the ferocity with which Buck Halliday had fought. It was still hard to believe that one man could have done so much damage to men, buildings and ambitions.

Henley stepped outside and went slowly along the street, glaring at the darkened windows as though they were mocking faces. When he returned to the saloon, he found the four men simply staring at him to see what he would say next.

'I may be beat,' he announced heavily, 'but, by hell, I'm not runnin'.'

He gave Mitchener a look of disgust and took another bottle of whiskey from the shelf behind the counter.

'I guess you better have this after all,' he said bitterly, 'or you're gonna fall apart at the seams by the look of you. But if you don't take it easy and stay outta trouble, so help me, I'll run you outta town myself. Speakin' of trouble, where's Julie? Anybody seen her since mornin'?'

'The last time I saw her, she was with the banker,' Shelton informed him.

'That's wonderful,' Henley roared. 'As if it ain't enough to have you bums turn me into a laughing-stock, I've got a wife that behaves worse than an alley cat. I don't suppose one of you brave boys might be so kind as to go and get her and drag her back where she belongs?'

Shelton hitched at his gunbelt and left the room, going straight up the street to the bank. It was closed, but Shelton could see the banker inside, working over a ledger by the light of a lamp.

He pounded on the window with the palm of his hand and demanded to be let in.

'Open the door, Carrigan,' he said, 'or I'll have to shoot my way in.'

The banker set down his pen and came to the door with his keys in his hand. He looked more annoyed than frightened.

'You know the bank's closed,' he said impatiently as he opened the door. 'What's so important that it can't wait till morning?'

'Henley's wife,' Shelton said. 'Where is she?'

Carrigan shook his head.

'She isn't here.'

'She was with you. So don't lie to me.'

'I told you she isn't here. I let her rest in the office for a while when she was so upset and didn't have anywhere else to go.'

Shelton seemed uncertain of what to do next. He continued to stare at the banker, and then he said again, 'She was with you.'

'I've already admitted as much!' Carrigan snapped. 'But I'll thank you to leave now. I have work to do.'

Shelton scowled, and then he said, 'Don't you try to tell me what to do, mister. No matter what happened today, things are just the same as ever in this town – and don't you think otherwise.'

With a sigh, the banker returned to his ledger and picked up his pen.

'Hey, I ain't finished with you yet,' Shelton said. 'If Mrs Henley ain't here, where did she go?'

'I don't know and I don't care!' Carrigan snapped. 'Now if you don't mind, I've work to do.'

Shelton began to clump back and forth in the silent building, making as much noise as possible as he checked the tellers' cages and the back rooms. When he finally returned, Carrigan looked up at him with a wry smile.

'Satisfied?'

'For now. But while I'm at it, get this straight and

spread it around all you like. Henley ain't beat, not while I'm alive and backin' him. Like I said before, nothin's gonna change in this town. It's just that I'm takin' over where Rafe left off. As for you, mister, you better start showin' some respect or you're gonna end up wearin' that there ledger around your jug ears.'

Pointedly, Shelton rested his hand on his gun butt.

'I . . . I don't want any trouble,' the banker assured him.

That seemed to satisfy Shelton, and he swaggered outside, leaving the door open behind him.

His next stop was the rooming house. There was a new man at the desk, a thin-faced individual who had come west on doctor's orders because of a weak chest. He had been clerking off and on at the feed store, but the dust was bad for his lungs and the light work at the rooming house suited him better. Besides, he was a great reader, and there was plenty of time for that in the new job.

'Yes?' he inquired as he looked up at Shelton while using one finger to keep his place in the novel he was reading.

'I'm tryin' to find Mrs Henley,' Shelton said.

'I'm awfully sorry,' the clerk said, 'but I haven't seen her.'

The news was disappointing, but Shelton liked the respectful way the clerk answered him.

*

After Buck Halliday left Shimmer Creek, he went to the spot on the creek where he had stopped on his way into town. He let his horse drink and went a few feet upstream to fill his canteen.

He was thinking about the town and the job he had just left behind. He was satisfied that he had earned his money, and he believed that even the judge would eventually admit that it was a job well done.

It left a sour taste in his mouth, though, to think that Cowper was blaming him for the bloodshed and that his niece had not even tried to disguise her revulsion for his line of work.

It was too early to make camp, but Halliday could see no sense in riding out so close to dark. He decided on a siesta, first unsaddling the horse and then finding himself a shady spot where he could stretch out with his hat over his eyes.

For a long time, he simply stared up into the sweat-stained crown of his hat and let his mind wander.

He was not sure how long he had dozed, but when he awoke, the sun was dropping behind the hills. His horse was standing hock-deep in the creek, seemingly bored by the inactivity. As soon as Halliday stirred, the sorrel came to him, dripping water.

'OK, boy,' Halliday said, 'you win.'

He pulled up a double handful of long grass and used it to rub the horse down until the coat gleamed like silk.

For the life of him, he could not feel any enthusiasm for going on.

In the short time he had known Cowper and his niece, he had come to respect them. They were good, honest people.

He saddled the horse again and started back toward Shimmer Creek. The darkness did not trouble him now that he knew the way, but he could remember no time when he had felt so uneasy about approaching a town.

He rode into the main street and saw that although it was not late, the street was almost empty. Lights showed in almost every window. It looked like folks were content to stay home tonight. . . .

Despite Jason Henley's clear warning, Lee Mitchener was getting drunk. Stuck in the saloon with only Tom Bassett and Ben Albert for company, he had soon finished off a bottle of whiskey on his own.

Only a handful of towners had visited the saloon all day, and the usual late afternoon rush had not materialized. Henley had not come downstairs all afternoon, and Luke Shelton seemed to be rushing around town like a blue-tailed fly, showing every sign of turning into a brash young gun brat. Mitchener was worried about Shelton. He had never liked the young man, and now he was beginning to understand why.

Rising from the card table, Mitchener walked lazily across the room and put the empty bottle down on the counter. Turning his back to the bar, he was tired of the saloon, the company and himself.

It was no improvement when Shelton strolled through the back door, but at least he might be capable of conversation. Bassett and Albert were never ones for small talk, and now they had sunk into moody silence.

'This is gonna drive me crazy,' Mitchener said to no one in particular. 'Many more days like this, and I'll be fit to bust.'

Shelton glanced at him without comment, but that was enough for Mitchener to move down the bar in his direction.

Neither of the two men spoke for some time. Mitchener now had a restricted view of the yard behind the saloon, but that was every bit as bleak and uninteresting as the almost-empty interior.

Shelton finally broke the silence when he drawled, 'Is the boss still upstairs?'

'All damn afternoon,' Mitchener said.

Shelton nodded in a reasonably friendly way, and Mitchener got the impression that he was loosening up a little.

'What do you figure he's doin' up there?' Shelton

inquired after another pause.

'Hard to say. Layin' his plans, most likely. I guess we'll find out when he's ready. I wonder who he's gonna get to take Murchison's place – did he tell you?'

Shelton nodded and looked pleased to be the one who knew.

'Ben Crowe,' he muttered.

Mitchener frowned and shook his head.

'Crowe'll cost him plenty. That feller don't come cheap.'

'Henley reckons it'll be worth it to pull this town back into line. You know Crowe, do you?'

'Hard to say,' Mitchener shrugged.

'What's that supposed to mean?'

'Well, I seen him cut down the Dakin boys at Indian Wells. That must be two years ago now. I was sittin' with him one afternoon at the same table in the saloon, and he never said a damn word, hardly even grunted. It was like sittin' with a dead man, only the ones that was dead was the Dakin brothers and Clem Grant who rode with them.'

'Fast, is he?' Shelton asked.

'Real fast. I was there to back him, but I never even had to draw my gun. Crowe just walked up to Jesse Dakin and told him to draw. Got him with one bullet. Bart Dakin come runnin', and he never even had time to pull his trigger. Grant come at him with a shotgun, but Crowe beat him to the trigger, too.

I'll tell you one thing, Henley won't have to spend much on bullets with that feller around. He got those three at Indian Wells with just three shots, no more.'

Shelton licked his lips and returned to the back door.

'He'll be comin' day after tomorrow on the stage,' he volunteered. 'Henley says he prefers to travel in style.'

'Crowe don't prefer nothin' but killin', believe you me. Take my advice and watch your step when he gets here. He don't like nothin' or nobody.'

Shelton nodded and went to sit on the back step.

Mitchener decided to follow him and keep him talking, but the young ranny had a moody look on his face now which seemed to be designed to discourage further conversation.

Mitchener sat down beside him anyway, and offered him the makings after he had rolled himself a cigarette.

Shelton shook his head and continued to stare blankly at the weed-grown yard.

'Somethin' eatin' you?' Mitchener asked finally.

It took so long for Shelton to speak that Mitchener was about to give up on him, but then he said;

'As a matter of fact, there is. It's that Cowper girl. The way she struts around with her nose in the air, I figure she's just askin' for it. And I'd sure like to oblige her.'

'You and me both,' Mitchener replied, his voice tinged with a healthy dose of lust.

Shelton looked up at Jason Henley's window.

'I sure am tired of doin' nothin',' he said. 'How about you?'

Mitchener looked up at the lighted window, too, and then he shrugged.

'You wanna go callin' on Beth Cowper, you mean?'

'Why not?'

Mitchener was thoughtful for a moment, then he grinned back at Shelton.

'Yeah,' he said. 'Why not. . . ? Henley won't mind. Tom and Ben can hold the fort.'

'Sure they can,' Shelton agreed as he got to his feet and settled the gunrig around his hips.

There were a couple of townsmen on the board-walk, but when they saw Mitchener and Shelton coming toward them side by side, they judiciously crossed the street.

'The lights are still on,' Mitchener observed when the Cowper house came into sight.

'Good,' Shelton grinned. 'It wouldn't be polite to wake somebody up just to make a social call, would it?'

With a careless glance back at the street, Shelton opened the gate and stepped into the yard.

'You knock on the door and I'll go around the

back,' he said.

Mitchener hesitated, but when Shelton disappeared around the corner of the house, he slowly mounted the front steps and rapped on the front door. He heard movement inside, and then Judge Cowper called;

'Who is it?'

Mitchener clapped a hand across his mouth and mumbled, 'Got a message for you, Judge, from Mr Halliday.'

There was a long moment's silence, and Mitchener saw the curtains twitch at the front window. Taking care to stay out of the light, Mitchener said, 'It's important, Judge.'

The curtains fell back into place, and Mitchener heard footsteps coming to the front door. He tipped his hat down to shade his face, and then he drew his gun and held it down at his side. When the door opened, he said quietly;

'Halliday said to tell you that . . . he ain't comin' back!'

Mitchener then let out a raucous laugh and pushed the old man back inside. He kicked the door closed as Beth Cowper rose with a gasp from the chair in the parlor corner where she had been doing some mending. The sewing basket fell to the floor, spilling pins and spools of thread at her feet.

The judge put his hand against the wall to steady

himself. He was trying to tell Beth to run, but then Shelton was running into the room from the kitchen and blocking her only avenue of escape.

She kicked out at him as he grabbed for her, but he only laughed and pinned her arms. She continued to struggle, but Shelton seemed to enjoy that.

'I do like a gal with spirit,' he grated. 'Who would've thought this one'd be such a spitfire, huh, Lee?'

The judge tottered shakily toward his niece, but Shelton lifted Beth and swung her so that her thrashing legs collided with the old man and knocked him to the floor. Cowper got up again with surprising speed and reached for Shelton.

The young gunnie danced away, still holding Beth in front of him and laughing at the old man's efforts to reach him.

Mitchener was simply watching it all with mild amusement, until he saw the judge veer away and reach for the top drawer of the cabinet beside Beth's chair.

Mitchener dived after him and slammed the drawer shut on his outstretched hand. Then he raised his six-gun, butt-first, and brought it down hard on the judge's skull.

Cowper grabbed for the cabinet as he fell, and the lamp Beth had been using for her mending, rocked and then toppled to the floor, the spilled oil igniting in a pool of flame.

Shelton threw Beth aside and swept up a rug to smother the flames.

'Dammit, Lee!' Shelton yelled. 'Help me put the fire out!'

Mitchener ran for the kitchen and Shelton continued to beat at the flames with the rug until Beth jumped at him from behind, hitting and kicking at him with all her strength. Shelton shook her off, then turned to face her. She came at him again, reaching for his eyes, but he sent her flying across the room with one hard punch.

Mitchener was back now and beating at the last of the flames with a broom. When the fire was out, the two men stepped back and surveyed the damage. The room was filled with smoke. Everyone was coughing, even the old man and the girl although they both appeared to be unconscious.

'I reckon we need some fresh air in here,' Mitchener said, and he went to open the windows and doors.

'Yeah,' Shelton said, 'now we can get back to the party. Let's just see where the guest of honor's gone. . . .'

He lifted Beth to her feet and carried her limp body to the sofa. Her eyelids fluttered but did not open.

Mitchener wiped his smoke-stained face on his sleeve and went to stand beside Shelton. He looked down at the girl and then said, 'We're makin' too much commotion, Luke. Somebody's gonna notice.'

'So what? Who's gonna stop us?'

Mitchener looked down at Beth again and saw that she was regaining consciousness. He wiped his hand across his mouth and said, 'It looks like the little lady's wakin' up.'

'It's a good thing, too,' Shelton grinned. 'I sure wouldn't want her to miss out on any of the fun – c'mon now, Miss Beth, open those pretty eyes of yours!'

He dragged her to her feet and shook her until he saw her focus on the horror that had taken over her parlor.

Shelton snickered in anticipation, but Beth suddenly broke away from him and clawed at his face. Shelton grabbed her blouse and tore it all the way down, leaving the girl's naked shoulders gleaming in the room's soft light.

Mitchener closed in from the other side, no longer uncertain. He felt a stirring in his loins at the sight of Beth's nakedness, and he reached for the flimsy lace that still covered her breasts. The garment came away in his hands, and he looked lasciviously at her as she tried to cover herself with her arms.

Shelton pushed her toward Mitchener, and they began to pass her back and forth between them, groping at her flinching body whenever she came within reach.

Beth found that she could not scream. Her throat seemed paralyzed by terror.

Then Mitchener put both arms around her and held her tight as he clamped his wet mouth over hers.

Beth struggled weakly in his grasp, but then Shelton dragged her clear and started to complain.

'Now hold on there, Lee – just remember, I'm in on this, too.'

'You bide your time, mister. There's enough of her for both of us.'

They returned to the game of jostling and pushing her from hand to hand. The room started to spin in front of her eyes, and she would have fallen if they had let her.

She struck out blindly at them, but they only continued to fondle her and tear at the remnants of her clothing.

Finally, she was naked and so exhausted that she could no longer stand. She closed her eyes to blot out their leering looks, and her flesh shrank in terrified expectation.

Seconds passed and nothing happened. Slowly, she opened her eyes.

They were crowded close around her, devouring her with their eyes.

Shelton wiped his hand down his face and found blood on his stubby fingers.

'By hell, that's it, girl. You been paradin' yourself

around for months, and now you're gonna get what's comin' to you!'

His breathing became harsh and rapid, and Beth cowered against the wall in the fetal position.

'You know what's going to happen to you?' Beth hissed. 'They're going to butcher you like the pigs you are!'

'Only if they catch us,' Shelton sneered. Then he turned to Mitchener and said, 'Lee, get on the other side and hold her.'

Mitchener moved in hesitantly and Beth turned her attack on him, raking her broken nails down his face until he grabbed her and forced her up against the wall. Then he slapped her twice so that her head rocked on her shoulders and her eyes began to glaze.

Shelton pushed in, grabbed her throat and forced her head up. He clamped his mouth over hers, but with the last of her strength, Beth sank her teeth into his lower lip.

'Hellcat!' Shelton yowled as he jumped back with blood pouring from his lip.

Then he hit her with his closed fist, and all the noises began to recede – Mitchener's rough laughter, Shelton's cursing and Beth's own whimpering.

'So, who's gonna be first?' Mitchener was asking as Buck Halliday stepped through the open doorway.

'The pleasure's all mine,' Halliday snarled, and

the six-gun bucked in his hand.

He fired twice, slicing a furrow along Mitchener's neck and shattering the bones in his gun hand.

Mitchener bellowed like a branded maverick and fell to the floor at Beth's feet. The wound on his neck was projecting a steady flow of blood several inches into the air. Shelton jumped sideways, with his hand slashing down for his gun.

Contemptuously, Halliday waited for him to clear leather. Then he pumped three bullets into him, punching a neat line across his chest. Shelton was dead before he hit the tangle of charred rugs on the floor in front of him.

Halliday stepped forward and inspected the two bodies, his face twisted in disgust.

Then he turned to Beth and bent to touch her gently on the shoulder. When she did not stir, he picked her up and carried her down the hall to the room where she had gone on his first visit to the house.

He placed her on the bed and covered her bruised body with the blanket which had been folded over the back of a chair.

Quietly, he retraced his steps to the parlor and went to judge's side. He was surprised to find that the old man was still alive.

FIVE

AN ANGRY TOWN

Jason Henley rolled off the bed at the first sound of the shooting in the street. For a moment he was unsure of its direction, but by the second burst of gunfire, he knew that it was coming from the eastern end.

He grabbed his gunbelt, fastening it around his thick waist as he hurried down the stairs.

He found Tom Bassett and Ben Albert standing together at the bar, an empty bottle between them, and said;

'What the hell was all that shooting?'

Both men shrugged, and then Bassett muttered, 'Sounded like it come from down by the store.'

'Then go check it out – and where did Shelton and Mitchener go?'

Bassett looked stupidly at Albert, and when Albert failed to answer, he said, 'We ain't seen either one of 'em for a while now. They went outside and never come back. . . .'

'If they're behind that shooting, I'll skin them alive!' Henley said coldly. 'Find them and bring them back here.'

Bassett worked his gunbelt into a more comfortable position and reached for his glass, but Henley yelled, 'Dammit, leave that whiskey alone and get goin' – and don't cause any more trouble than you have to.'

Bassett heeled around and Albert slouched after him, both men displaying little enthusiasm for the chore.

The street outside was quiet, with a single knot of curious townsmen grouped in front of the general store. Bassett made his way across to them and asked roughly, 'Who was makin' all the noise?'

Nobody answered, but he caught the attention of two men whose gaze was fixed on the distant Cowper house.

'In the judge's place, was it?' Bassett growled.

Without answering, the townsmen began to drift away.

Bassett cursed them and started walking with Albert just behind him, checking his gun as he went.

'You smell smoke?' Bassett asked his companion.

'Yeah,' Albert said, 'but I sure don't see any.'

'I don't like this one damn bit,' Bassett whispered.

They were at the Cowpers' gate now, and Albert wiped his hands on his pants and drew his six-gun.

The two men went up the path together. When they saw that the door was open, they stopped and looked at each other. There was no sound coming from inside the house, but a lamp was burning somewhere down the hall.

'What the hell's goin' on, you think?' Bassett whispered.

'Only one way to find out, I guess,' Albert responded.

Halliday had helped the judge into a chair, and he was just bringing him a glass of brandy when he heard a foot scrape on the front porch.

He went quietly across the room to the wall beside the doorway and waited. He heard footsteps again and then a hesitant voice say, 'Lee? Luke? You boys in there?'

From their conversation, it appeared that the two men were unwilling to fully enter the house.

'Don't look like they're here, Tom. Let's take a look in back and get outta here. I don't like this one bit.'

'Looks like they ain't here, Ben.'

They were moving again to the edge of the porch when Halliday stepped into the doorway.

Bassett turned and lifted his gun. Albert was only a step in front of him, and he turned with a look of

75

profound surprise on his stubbled face.

'That's as far as you go, boys,' Halliday said quietly. 'Drop those guns right now or you'll die where you stand.'

Bassett's mouth hung slack.

'Halliday,' he grunted.

'Yeah, it's me. Now drop those guns.'

Bassett looked sidelong at Albert, who threw his six-gun into the yard. Instead, Bassett simply dropped his Colt back into his holster.

'We weren't makin' any trouble, Mr Halliday,' he said reasonably. 'We're just out lookin' for Lee and Luke. Thought they might be here, but I can see we're wrong.'

'You weren't wrong,' Halliday said icily. 'It's just that they're dead.'

Bassett's jaw dropped, and finally he managed to ask, 'Both of 'em, you mean?'

Halliday nodded.

'Yeah, both,' he said. 'They beat up the judge and tried to manhandle his niece. Then for some reason, they tried to set fire to the house.'

He moved forward without further comment and plucked Bassett's Colt from its holster. He emptied it and threw it into the front yard alongside Albert's gun.

Quite a number of neighbors had gathered at the gate now, and they heard Halliday ask, 'What're your names?'

Bassett looked to where his gun had been thrown and cursed under his breath.

'I'm Tom Bassett. This here's Ben Albert.'

'You must be just about the last of Henley's bunch, I'd guess?'

The two men nodded miserably, and then Bassett said, 'We never hurt anybody, Mr Halliday. Hell, all we was doing was earnin' an honest livin'.'

'There are other ways, you know.'

'Yeah, guess there is . . . but we was down on our luck, and all we been doin' for Henley is lookin' after the saloon. You can't blame us for all this other stuff. We never had a hand in it, and that's the truth.'

Halliday stared sourly at Bassett for several moments, and then he stood back and beckoned the two men inside.

'Judas!' Bassett whispered when he saw the scorch marks of the fire and the judge with his bloodied head.

'I know you had no part in this,' Halliday said as he pointed to the two corpses he had dragged into a corner of the room, 'but you rode with this scum, so you can be the ones to haul them out of here.'

Wordlessly, the two men rushed to the dead men and started to drag them out to the hallway.

Judge Cowper appeared to have been sitting there in a daze. Suddenly, he looked up and asked, 'What are you men doing here? Halliday? What's happened? Where's Beth?'

'Everything's OK, Judge. Little harm done. I've got a chore to do, and then I'll be back. You just stay here and take it easy.'

Halliday followed Bassett and Albert into the yard.

'OK,' he said, 'now keep movin' with that garbage. We don't want it here. Take it back to Henley, where it belongs.'

'Sure,' Albert hastened to say. 'We're goin' right now.'

'Another thing,' Halliday said.

'What's that?' Bassett asked quickly.

'This is your last day in this town,' he told them mildly. 'Next time I see you, I'll kill you. That's a promise.'

Bassett nodded and looked away.

'How about you, feller?' Halliday asked Albert. 'You got any argument with that?'

'Nope,' Albert said slowly. 'We're goin'.'

'And you're not comin' back.'

'We won't, Mr Halliday,' Albert insisted. 'We won't come back. Not never.'

'Yeah, that'll be soon enough,' Halliday said as he began to roll a cigarette.

'Mr Halliday?' Bassett asked tentatively.

'Yeah.'

'Can we get our guns?'

'Sure. Just be careful you don't shoot yourselves in the foot, you're shakin' so much.'

'Thanks, Mr Halliday.'

Dragging the dead men behind them, the two hardcases had gone several yards down the street by the time Halliday lit the cigarette and took his first puff.

It was only then that he holstered his gun.

That was what Bassett had been waiting for. He dropped Shelton's feet as though he was trying to get a fresh grip on them, and with his back turned, he hastily reloaded his gun. Then he came running back to the house, trying to get a bead.

As he charged through the knot of neighbors outside the judge's fence, someone stuck out a boot.

Bassett fell hard, and the gun discharged as it shot from his hand and bounced against a picket by the gate.

Halliday ambled down the path and picked up the gun, shaking his head.

'Didn't I tell you two to be careful with those guns? You damn near came close to shootin' yourself in the foot, Bassett. I'm goin' to have to confiscate this hogleg for your own good, I guess. Now get the hell outta here.'

Albert watched Bassett pick himself up, his face a flaming red.

'Albert?' Halliday called. 'Come back here and help your pard.'

Albert nodded and hurriedly returned to the judge's front gate.

'Why'd you go and do a thing like that, you

79

jughead?' Albert scolded Bassett. 'You wanna end up dead?'

'I thought you bums understood what I said,' Halliday complained wearily. 'A man only has so much patience and no more, you know.'

'We're goin', Mr Halliday,' Albert said grimly. 'If this idjut comes back, he'll be doin' it on his own. I've had enough of this, and I don't want no more.'

'Mighty sensible, mister.'

'Yeah,' Albert muttered as he dragged Tom Bassett back to the two corpses already stiffening on the edge of the street.

'I figure the excitement's all over now, folks,' Halliday told the neighbors as he sauntered back to the house. 'You might as well go on home.'

With some reluctance, the townspeople began to disperse. A few had come right into the yard and were peering in the front windows.

Judge Cowper was on his feet now, and he agreed with Halliday. 'Off you go now, folks. I have to talk to Mr Halliday here, in private.'

As soon as they were alone, Cowper said;

'I'm not sure what happened, Halliday. Two men busted in and grabbed Beth. When I went to get my gun, one of them knocked me out. Beth is still so . . . distraught that I can't get any sense out of her.'

Cowper's lips thinned and a pained look came into his eyes.

'Do you know how . . . bad it was, Halliday?

80

Heaven, if they so much as—'

'They didn't,' Halliday said quietly. 'I got here in time.'

Cowper breathed a sigh of relief.

'How can we ever thank you, Mr Halliday? After the way we treated you, what made you come back?'

'I'm not sure, Judge. Somethin' just felt like . . . unfinished business. I knew Henley wouldn't give up that easy, I guess.'

Cowper nodded.

'I certainly was wrong about that,' he said. 'I thought we could handle him, with Rafe gone. Now look what he's done. I'll never forgive him for what's happened to Beth. I'll get him for this, if it's the last thing I do!'

Halliday moved restlessly around the room, inspecting the damage to the floor and helping himself to a drink.

'I'll handle Henley, Judge,' he said finally. 'I started this and it should be up to me to finish it.'

'No,' Cowper insisted, 'you've done enough, too much even. This is personal, between him and me.'

'It's real nice to see you so full of fight, Judge,' Halliday said gently. 'But this ain't your kind of fight. You know better than I do that no court of law would blame him for what a couple drunken hired hands did. If the law operated like that, half the ranchers in this country would be in jail on account of somethin' their cowhands took it into their heads to do. You know what it takes to stop a man like Henley. You have to fight fire with fire. That's why you asked me to come here in the first place.'

Cowper looked at him thoughtfully.

'I just can't understand why you're willing to do this,' he said finally. 'I don't feel like we deserve it.'

Halliday smiled faintly. 'Put it down to loose ends, Judge. I like to ride away from a job knowin' that I've left everything nice and tidy. Shimmer Creek is still a long ways short of tidy – we both know that. It doesn't feel right to me.'

Halliday finished his drink and set down the empty glass. He was about to leave when Beth stepped quietly into the room.

She was wearing a simple cotton dress with long sleeves and a frilled high neck so that only the bruises on her face were showing. Her hair was brushed and tied back loosely with a satin bow.

Halliday removed his hat and gave her a small and respectful smile.

'You Cowpers sure are made of stern stuff. Neither one of you looks like you've been through anything worse than gettin' to bed a little late.'

'Thank you, Mr Halliday,' Beth said calmly. 'Did you kill those two men?'

The judge tried to interrupt, anxious to stop her if she was going to tell Halliday again that there was no excuse for his kind of violence.

Before he could speak, Halliday was giving his

answer in a flat, quiet voice.

'Yes.'

Beth ran the tip of her tongue over her lips and left them shining.

'I'm obliged to you more than I can ever express then, Mr Halliday. They were about to. . . .'

'I know what they were about to do.'

'Try not to think about it anymore, honey,' the judge said. 'I only wish I had been able to get to that gun before they knocked me out!'

'Mr Halliday,' Beth went on, 'when I came to again, I was on my bed and I was simply too frightened to move or think. What happened?'

Halliday shrugged.

'Two more of Henley's men turned up – but they won't bother either of you again.'

'You mean you killed them, too?' Beth asked softly.

'No. They've decided to leave town for good of their own accord.'

Halliday moved back a couple of paces, making it clear to them that he wanted to be on his way.

Beth glanced at the bundle of torn clothing laying on the sofa and realized she was looking at every stitch she had been wearing earlier in the evening.

Her cheeks reddened, and she went slowly to the sofa and scooped up the ragged bundle.

She stood in front of Halliday for a moment then, looking up at him earnestly.

'Thank you again, Mr Halliday,' she whispered.

Halliday nodded awkwardly, fitted his hat to his head and headed for the door.

SIX

THREATS AND PROMISES

'Mr Halliday.'

The call came from the alley beside the saloon. Buck Halliday stopped, his hand automatically dropping to his holster.

As his eyes adjusted to the darkness, he could see Julie Henley standing near the saloon wall. He did not know why, but he got the immediate impression that she had been there for some time.

'I saw what you did to Tom and Ben,' she said. 'They won't be back.'

'I'm not surprised, Mrs Henley.'

'My name is Julie,' she told him, and there was an edge of annoyance to her voice.

'As you like.'

Halliday began to move away, but she put out her hand and held onto his arm.

'What are you goin' to do now, Buck?'

'See your husband and give him some sound advice.'

'Are you goin' to kill him?'

'Not unless I have to.'

'You won't. He doesn't have the guts to stand up to anyone . . . let alone you. You've run rings around him and all his men. He's on his own now. Do you know what that means?'

'Tell me.'

Julie moved closer to him, and the scent from her soft hair tickled his nostrils. He looked down at her and saw the pleasure in her eyes.

'He's finished, Buck. You've beaten him. He's going to run away like a whipped dog. That's what he always does when somebody stands up to him. And this time, I'll have what he leaves behind.'

Julie moved out of the alley into the streetlight washing over Halliday's broad shoulders. Her face was turned up to him, and she seemed to be positively glowing with excitement.

Halliday was reminded of how she had looked as she lay on the bed in his room, but then another picture formed in his mind – Beth Cowper lying naked on her uncle's floor. He said, 'You intend to stay on then?'

'Yes, why not? My only worry in this town is my husband. With him out of the way, I can hire some capable men and make a good living running the saloon.'

Halliday eased her fingers from his arm and began to move away. Julie followed him and pressed herself against him.

'I want you with me, Buck. We can make ourselves rich with all the comforts. I'll be good for you, I promise.'

'I got things to do first,' Halliday shrugged. 'Then we might talk about it. You stay here. I want to see Henley on his own.'

'Whatever you say, Buck,' Julie said, but before he could step away from her, she planted a kiss on his unresponsive mouth.

Halliday stepped around her and cut down the alley to the back door of the saloon. When he entered the barroom, he saw that Jason Henley was waiting for him with his gun drawn.

Halliday glanced at him and went to lean against the counter.

'You're runnin' short of men, Henley,' he said tonelessly. 'Mitchener and Shelton are dead. Bassett and Albert have left town, and I don't reckon they'll be back.'

Henley shook his head in grim denial.

'You're lyin', damn you! They'll be back. They won't run out on me after all I've done for them.'

'What you've done for them, mister, is make sure everybody in this town is just itchin' to string them up. You're all on your own now and the town doesn't need you or want you. So I'm giving you half an hour to pack your things and get gone. If you're here after that, I'll come looking for you.'

Henley's hand was shaking, and his face was white from a combination of hate and anger.

'By hell, you're the one that's going to die, not me,' he snarled. 'You don't scare me. . . .'

'I'm givin' you a chance you don't deserve, mister,' Halliday said. 'What you do with it is your business.'

'A bullet'll stop you, same as it will any other man,' Henley snapped, and his finger tightened on the trigger.

Halliday continued to watch him, but there was no sign that he was concerned by the threat.

'Maybe you don't know that Mitchener and Shelton beat up Judge Cowper and tried to rape his niece. They came close to burnin' the judge's house down, too. When folks get wind of that, they'll come lookin' for you anyway. I don't figure they'd give you a chance to get out of town – they'd just string you up to the first tree they came to.'

Henley took a step back, torn between hatred and fear.

'I hear your wife will be stayin' on and takin' over the saloon, so you don't need to worry about her future,' Halliday said as he went to the batwings and glanced out at the town clock. 'Half an hour, mister. Startin' now.'

Henley was shaking with rage now, and Halliday decided that he had pushed the man far enough. He simply folded his arms and waited to see what Henley would do.

Henley still had the gun he had been holding when Halliday walked into the barroom, and now he simply raised it and fired. The bullet nicked Halliday's shoulder, but before Henley could fire again, Halliday had struck a sledging blow to the man's neck and kicked the gun from his hand.

Henley was backing desperately away now and trying to shield his face with his hands, but Halliday followed and drove him across the room with a series of stinging blows.

The saloon man was beginning to buckle at the knees, but Halliday grabbed him by the front of his shirt and dragged him up the stairway to the rooms above the saloon.

'Ready to start packin' now, mister?' Halliday asked calmly. 'You're runnin' out of time, you know.'

Snorting and gasping through his swollen nose, Henley stumbled into a room with an open door and pulled a carpetbag from under the brass bed.

Then he simply stood there with his head hanging and the empty bag dangling from his fingers.

'I . . . I don't know where to start,' he muttered.

'Well, I'll tell you,' Halliday said. 'Pack enough clothes to get you at least as far as Kansas. And you can take a hundred dollars in foldin' money, no more. Anything above that is gonna get handed back to the folks you've been bleedin' dry.'

Henley sagged against the wall, wiping blood from his face. He fingered his swollen jaw, and then he began to pull shirts and collars out of a chest of drawers.

'Damn you to hell, Halliday,' he said in an exhausted voice.

'Pack,' Halliday ordered. 'You've still got one other thing to do before you get out of here, and time's a-wastin'.'

'What other thing?' Henley asked dully.

'I want you to sign everything you own over to your wife.'

Finally, the carpetbag was full and the papers had been signed. Henley sighed and fished in his vest pocket until he came up with a small brass key. He fitted the key in the lock of the top drawer.

As his hand dipped into the drawer and his shoulders bunched, Halliday stepped across the room and slammed the drawer on Henley's wrist. Then he hurled the man across the room. When Henley hit the wall, Halliday turned and looked in the drawer, rummaging through the papers and small change until he found the little sneak gun wrapped in a linen handkerchief.

'You just don't know when to quit, do you?' Halliday said with a shake of his head.

Henley was propped against the wall now, watching him but making no attempt to move.

'I wonder what else there is in here?' Halliday said as he returned to pawing through the contents. 'Hey, this looks kind of interestin' – a locked box inside a locked drawer. Love letters, are they?'

Henley watched helplessly as Halliday smashed the box against the brass bed until the lock was sprung. The box was packed so tightly with banknotes that the money stayed in place when he upended the box.

'More like keepsakes, I guess,' Halliday grinned. 'I guess all these presidents are heroes of yours, huh?'

He peeled a hundred dollars off the top and tossed it to Henley.

'Come on now,' he said as he grabbed Henley by the shoulder and pushed him toward the door. 'You got a long ways to go, and you better get started.'

When they reached the yard, Halliday stood back and watched while Henley saddled a horse.

'OK,' he said as the man placed his foot in the stirrup. 'Off you go now. I purely hate long goodbyes. Just keep one thing in mind – if you come back, I'll be waitin' for you.'

Henley looked down at him bitterly.

'You might like to think you can call the shots,' he said, 'but your kind can never stick it out for long.

You have to have somebody do the thinking and give the orders. I'll be back to prove it to you, if it's the last thing I do.'

'It'll be the last thing you try, mister,' Halliday said flatly. 'Now get the hell out of my sight.'

Henley glanced back at his saloon and caught sight of his wife, standing on the bottom step to watch him go. He gave no sign that he had seen her, but he nudged his horse into a walk that would take him right past the back porch.

When he reached her, Julie looked up at him and said, 'You just weren't good enough, were you? Not even with a gun in your hand. Now we both know how spineless you are.'

Henley had reined-in the horse, but now he nudged it with his heels and reached out at the same time to grab at Julie's hair.

Halliday was there before the woman could open her mouth to scream, and the six-gun was in his hand.

'Let her go,' he said simply.

Henley opened his hand, and the woman stepped back and pushed her hair out of her eyes.

He looked over his shoulder at Halliday and then he turned to his wife again.

'I'm nowhere near finished with you,' he hissed. 'You'll find that out. I'll be back for you, and soon. Either I'll tame you, or I'll see you dead. You're still my goddamn wife.'

He kicked the horse into a run, and when it shot out of the alley, someone on the boardwalk recognized him.

'Look who's leavin' town, pards! See? He's got his belongin's all packed up in that bag.'

'More likely it's our belongin's,' someone answered, and suddenly a crowd was gathering.

Henley saw the signs and slapped the reins.

Buck Halliday was sitting at the bar and Julie was standing behind it to refill his glass when the judge walked through the batwings, moving with the energy and purpose of a much younger man.

Several townsmen clustered just outside the batwing doors but seemed unwilling to cross the threshold.

'Mrs Henley,' the judge greeted Julie, and then he fetched up at the bar beside Halliday.

'I'll get straight to the point,' he told Halliday.

'Good idea, Judge. I've a hankerin' for some peace and quiet.'

'Mr Halliday, I've had a long talk with my niece and some of the city fathers. There's still lots to do here in Shimmer Creek, and we figure you're the man for the job.'

'My job for you is done, Judge,' Halliday told him flatly.

'I'm talking about something else,' the judge said. 'We think there could be a permanent position here for you. Without Henley draining us dry, this town is all set to grow into something prosperous and decent . . . but it has to have some law.'

Halliday gave no sign that he heard.

The judge seemed annoyed by Julie's presence. He turned a little away from her and lowered his voice.

'Do you understand what I'm saying, Mr Halliday? We're asking you to be our sheriff.'

Halliday was looking straight at Julie, and she was the one who answered for him.

'You're too late, Judge.'

'Oh?' Cowper asked absently, still concentrating his attention on Halliday. 'You've decided to leave?'

'He's decided to stay and work for me,' Julie told him.

'You mean you are taking over the saloon, Mrs Henley?' Cowper asked.

'Yes. And I've hired Buck to help me run it.'

Cowper could not hide his disappointment as he stepped back from the bar.

'That's regrettable,' he muttered, still keeping his eyes on Halliday, 'but I suppose I have only myself to blame. I should've trusted your judgment all along instead of trying to tell you how to handle something I knew so little about. Anyway, I want you to know this town is beholden, and no one could be more grateful than me, Mr Halliday.'

Cowper extended his hand, and Halliday gripped it.

'Like I said,' Halliday told him, 'I've been paid for what I did. But it's nice to hear what you just said. It's mighty unusual for a feller in my line of work to hear that kind of praise after the job is done. There's always lots of glad-handin' beforehand, but folks have a tendency to turn kinda frosty when they don't need you no more.'

The judge nodded Julie's way and added, 'I wish you luck, Mr Halliday, and the sheriff's job is still there if you happen to change your mind. All you have to do is let me know.'

'Thanks,' Halliday said as the judge headed for the door.

Over the batwings, he could see Cowper in conversation with the men waiting on the boardwalk. After a few minutes, the bunch moved away.

Julie pushed another drink across the counter and said, 'It's gettin' late, Buck. I'll fix a room for you upstairs.'

Halliday shook his head.

'The rooming house suits me just fine.'

'Why? Now that everything's settled—'

'You don't believe that anymore than I do. He'll be back.'

'Of course he won't. When he said those things, he was just tryin' to cover his shame.'

'He'll ride back in a day or so and I want to be ready for him and whoever he brings with him. I want no complications until this thing with your husband is settled once and for all.'

Julie filled her glass and emptied it just as quickly.

'What time in the mornin', boss?' Halliday asked quietly.

'I'll open up when it suits me.'

'I'll check in at nine o'clock then,' Halliday told her, closing the doors on his way out.

When he was back in his room, he shrugged out of his shirt and examined the nick Henley's bullet had left along his shoulder. He filled the basin and cleaned the graze. Then he found the whiskey bottle and splashed a little of the reddish-brown liquid into the palm of his hand and wiped his hand over the raw skin.

He winced as he replaced the cork in the bottle. Then he thought better of it and took a long swallow.

He was tired and certain that Henley would not be back so soon. This was one time when even the lovely Julie Henley was no competition for a good night's sleep.

Beth Cowper was waiting on the front porch when her uncle returned. As soon as she saw the disappointment in his face, she said, 'Something has gone wrong, hasn't it?'

'Mr Halliday has other plans, Beth,' the old man said gently.

'He's leaving?'

'No.'

'What then?' Beth asked.

Cowper did not answer until he had splashed whiskey into a glass and had taken two fortifying sips. Then he said, 'Jason Henley has left town, and Julie Henley has taken over the running of the saloon. Halliday is going to work for her.'

Beth was shocked.

'But she's . . . she's. . . .'

'I know,' Cowper said. 'And maybe Halliday knows it, too. Anyway, it's not for us to judge, Beth. They have their own lives to lead. The thing is, though, Mr Halliday will still be in our town. That in itself gives me a great deal of hope for the future. We'll just have to manage as best we can without his services.'

While he talked, Cowper studied his niece and knew she was no longer listening to him. He paused for awhile, and then said, 'He's done us all a fine service, Beth, but the fact still remains that he is no more than a hired gun. He will never belong to any one place or any one woman. One day, he will tire of this town and he will simply get on his horse and go.'

Beth looked up angrily and snapped, 'What Buck Halliday chooses to do is no concern of mine! Good night, Uncle. It's late and I'm going to bed.'

'Good night, Beth,' Cowper said, and watched her flounce out of the room.

When her door closed harder than it usually did,

he dropped into a chair.

It might be a relief to know that his sweet and innocent niece would not be getting any closer to a man like Buck Halliday, but the judge knew that he would be losing her before long to some man. She was a grown woman with many fine qualities, although probably a little too independent for most men's taste.

When the time came, the house was going to seem empty.

Cowper's head drooped. He felt suddenly old and – what was the word he wanted. . . ?

Expendable.

SEVEN

WAITING FOR THE MAN

Jason Henley rode all night. Staying awake when the world was in darkness was no problem to a man who had been running a saloon, but the long hours in the saddle left him stiff and sore.

The sun was just starting to appear when he approached the long stretch of desert serviced by a weekly stage run which made the round trip between Shimmer Creek and Layton.

Henley was planning to wait for the stage that would be heading for Shimmer Creek – the one that would be carrying Ben Crowe. He wanted to make sure that the gunman knew the deal to kill Buck Halliday still stood, despite the dramatic changes at

Shimmer Creek.

He came stiffly out of the saddle and led his horse into the weak shade provided by the spindly trees that struggled to survive on the edge of the desert, and then he sank to the ground and pulled off his boots so that he could work the cramp out of his feet.

A faint scraping noise came from somewhere behind him, and he rose on his haunches and grabbed at his holster. That was when he remembered that he had no gun.

Sweat broke out on his forehead as he scanned the empty landscape. It seemed that the noise must have come from the shallow arroyo – there was no other place of concealment. Maybe it was just a Gila monster or a snake.

Henley had just about decided that the noise was nothing of any importance when Tom Bassett led his horse out of the arroyo, with Ben Albert behind him.

They seemed to hesitate when they saw Henley, but they finally dismounted and came over to him.

'You weak-livered bums ran out on me!' Henley snapped.

'Seems like you're doin' some runnin' of your own, Mr Henley,' Bassett growled. ' 'Less maybe you just come out here for a change of scenery.'

Henley scowled back at him but let it go at that.

'Halliday ran me out of town,' he explained. 'If there'd been the three of us, we might've been able

100

to stop him, but I couldn't do it on my own.'

'Not likely,' Albert said bluntly. 'The three of us wouldn't have been enough to go up against Halliday. Look what he did to the others that you had on your payroll.'

'He's only one man,' Henley growled.

'Try tellin' that to him,' Albert muttered, scratching idly at the dirt with a sharp-edged pebble.

His eyes were on the desert, and it was clear from his expression that he was looking at something he did not like. Years before, he had barely lived through a similar crossing, and the agony of it still burned into his memory.

Ever since the day he had staggered onto the trail where he was rescued, he had never been able to think of sand without remembering how it had felt to be covered in a skin of raw blisters and so crazy with thirst that he tried to drink his own sweat.

Henley studied each of the men in turn for a moment before he barked, 'What's done is done. I know that, but I'd still like to know what the hell happened to you two back at Shimmer Creek. I sent you to find Lee and Luke, and you didn't come back. Halliday turned up at the saloon instead. If I'd had some warning—'

'Halliday was in Cowper's home when we got there,' Albert told him. 'He'd just gunned down Lee and Luke for roughin' up the judge and his niece. When we showed up, he made us drag Lee and Luke outside, and then he told us to get outta town. Tom bucked him at the last minute, and you can see what he got for his trouble. I don't want no part of Halliday, not today, not next week, not ever.'

Henley scowled and then turned to Bassett.

'What's your version of all this?'

Bassett fingered his swollen jaw, and said, 'Just about the same, I guess. Only that I might've had a better chance against Halliday if I'd had somebody to back me up.'

Albert wiped his palms down his dusty pants and looked at each of them in turn.

'A man that tangles with Halliday is askin' for everythin' he gets, Tom. Hell, you didn't stand a chance. Neither of us did, not even together. He don't lose out . . . never.'

'We could've got him once and for all,' Bassett insisted, 'but you just sat back and wouldn't lift a finger.'

'There was nothin' I could do. Hell, he had his gun out, and anybody could see it was loco to go for him – anybody but you, that is. What you done was plain foolish, and I ain't a fool.'

Bassett turned his head and hawked. Henley noticed that he was favoring his right side and one ear was swollen to almost twice its usual size.

'Well,' Henley said, 'whatever you fellers have to say about it, Halliday ain't makin' me leave. I've worked too hard to get my hands on that town, and

I'm going back, just as soon as Crowe turns up. I'm going to see Halliday dead. After that, I aim to teach that wife of mine a lesson she won't forget.'

'You really mean to go back there, do you?' Bassett asked.

'Ain't that what I just said?' Henley snapped. 'Ben Crowe is the fastest gun that ever came out of the Platte River country. He's also mean as a snake, and he takes pride in bein' the top man wherever he goes. I'm payin' him plenty to take Halliday out. Ben won't let me down, not like some.'

Bassett nodded his head gravely, and then he turned to Albert.

'What do you say, Ben? You still ridin' with us or not?'

Albert shook his head vigorously.

'I sure as hell ain't. I seen way too much of Halliday already, and I don't know nothin' about Crowe except that any man's a fool who takes on Halliday. If you want to have Halliday beatin' up on you again, that's your business. Just as soon as the sun goes down, I'm pushing on to Layton.'

'You're that scared of Halliday?' Bassett said heavily.

'You damn betcha I am, an' I don't mind admittin' it. And if Halliday didn't scramble your brains so bad you can't see sense, you'll be comin' right along with me. In Layt—'

'Shut up, damn you!' Henley roared. 'Ain't

nobody running out on me again. You're both goin' back to Shimmer Creek with me, and we're going to see that Ben Crowe gets his chance at Halliday. I want that town to see Halliday go down. It's the only way to bring those fools back into line.'

Albert wiped a line of sweat from his face and shook his head. 'No, Henley, I'm all through with this. You had nine men backin' you against Halliday, and we all saw what happened. He cut them to ribbons. Can't you get it through your head? Throwin' a scare into a bunch of storekeepers is one thing . . . Halliday's somethin' else.'

Henley looked up at the cloudless sky.

It was Bassett who responded to Albert's outburst.

'I'll lay it out nice and simple, Ben,' he said. 'Either you throw in with us, or you can walk to Layton, 'cause I'll be takin' that horse of yours.'

Albert looked from Bassett to Henley like a cornered animal.

'Tom,' he said, 'you can't say I let you down at Shimmer Creek. You just took on somethin' that was too big for you. All I can say is you're damn lucky that Halliday let you live. The best thing you can do is forget all about it – we could have us a real nice time down along the border. What do you say to that?'

Henley stooped down and picked up a large, flat rock. Bassett saw his move and kept Albert talking.

'You got a hankerin' for Mexico, huh?'

'I sure do. All that spicy food and hot women. Everything's cheap down there, Tom. Why, it hardly costs—'

Henley hit him just behind the right ear. Albert let out a grunt and fell flat. There was no sign of movement, but Henley bent down and hit him again. Blood began to flow from the shattered skull, and a line of ants appeared from nowhere as if they had been waiting for a man to leak a little his blood.

'He was nothing but a coward,' Henley said as he looked up to see Bassett's reaction to what he had done.

'Don't bother me none,' Bassett said with a shrug. 'I told you how he let me down.'

Henley nodded.

'I'm going to remember how you stood by me today, Tom,' Henley said. 'You won't be sorry.'

Bassett nodded and proceeded to drag Albert's body away by the heels, dumping it in the arroyo and kicking dirt from the bank on top of it.

Julie Henley hired two men to look after the saloon, and they were sweeping and scrubbing while she took stock of the finances in the upstairs office.

She was overjoyed to discover that her husband had stocked up with enough whiskey to last out a long, hot summer.

She had found his little sneak gun and a couple of crumpled banknotes in the room. There also was a badly dented tin box, but it was empty and she assumed that her husband had cleaned it out.

Maybe there was little cash on hand, but things looked good, especially with Buck Halliday beside her. She was sure that he would not remain so stand-offish for long, and she considered that it was well worth waiting for a man like that.

Humming to herself, she locked the room behind her and went down the stairs.

She was pleased to find that everything was back in shape and Josh Harper was all set up behind the bar, waiting for the day's first customers.

'Has Mr Halliday been in yet, Josh?' Julie asked with a pleasant smile.

'No, Mrs Henley,' the new barkeep answered. 'Ain't seen hide nor hair of him.'

'When he comes in, tell him I want to see him, will you?' Julie said, and after another look around the quiet saloon, she went upstairs again, this time to her own room.

She opened the windows and looked down on the street with all the affection of a proud new owner. To make things even better, she spotted Halliday heading for the business block.

She had her head out the window and was ready to wave and call his name when she saw him tip his hat to none other than Beth Cowper.

'Damn!' Julie whispered as she stepped back from the window.

She went to her bed and straightened the pillows and the coverlet, but then found herself back at the window.

Halliday was still there, talking amiably with Beth and her uncle.

Even from a distance, she could see that the meeting was friendly from all sides.

Finally, she slammed the window down, but she could not bring herself to turn away. Then she saw Halliday reach inside his shirt and bring out a bulky package, which he handed to the judge.

From the way the judge opened a corner of the package and put it quickly inside his coat, Julie was suddenly certain that Halliday had just handed the old man a great deal of money.

In one quick moment of realization, Julie knew who had emptied that tin box in the office.

She hurried out of the room and went downstairs to the barroom.

Four customers had arrived, and they were talking and joking with Harper as they waited for him to pour the first drinks of the day.

Ignoring the customers, Julie went straight up to Harper and said, 'Mr Halliday is in the street now, Josh. Would you go tell him I want to see him right away?'

'Sure, Mrs Henley,' Harper said, and pulled off the apron and left it on the counter.

When he reached the street, he saw that Halliday

was already on his way to the saloon.

'The boss lady wants to see you,' he said. 'And she's actin' like there's a bee in her bonnet.'

Halliday nodded but instead of going straight to the saloon, he sauntered toward the livery stable. It was a good half an hour later when he finally pushed his way through the batwings.

Julie was waiting for him, with an angry spot of color flaming on each cheekbone.

'Well, it's awfully nice of you to finally show up for work,' she said sharply. 'I suppose you had more important things on your mind, did you?'

'As a matter of fact, I did. My horse, for one thing.'

'And the Cowper girl, I suppose?'

'What are you gettin' at, Julie?' Halliday asked quietly.

'I saw you in the street . . . with her.'

'If you have somethin' to say to me, spit it out,' Halliday said impatiently.

'Yes, I do have somethin' to say, Buck. I've got big plans for us – wonderful plans – and I don't want half the town laughin' at me behind my back.'

'What are you talkin' about now?' Halliday demanded.

'I'm talkin' about us, Buck, what else? You know I'm twice the woman that mealy-mouthed Beth Cowper is . . . and I want you to stay away from her.'

'Hold on a minute, Mrs Hen—'

'Don't call me that. I told you never to call me by that name again, ever!'

Halliday waited for her anger to subside, then he answered her in a firm, quiet voice.

'You hired me to do a job for you ... to keep thing's runnin' smooth in the saloon, that's all.'

Julie drew herself rigidly to her full height. She was strikingly beautiful and mad as hell.

'I want you,' she said flatly, 'and I'm willin' to share everything I've got to have you for my own, Buck Halliday.'

Halliday looked at her uneasily. The drinkers at the bar were being careful not to look their way, but their ears were just about burning.

Julie had the kind of body that could turn strong men into boys, and there was no doubt that she had the spunk to stand up to Jason Henley and spit in his eye. For Halliday, the trouble was that she was not Beth Cowper.

'You've got yourself all het up over nothin',' Halliday said finally. 'All things considered, I don't think workin' for you is such a good idea after all. I'm sorry, but you'll just have to get yourself another man.'

Julie stared at him in open-mouthed shock, and then she slapped his face with all the strength she could muster.

She saw his eyes narrow in anger, and she involuntarily took a step back, knowing that she had gone too far.

109

A moment passed, and then Halliday looked down at her. His face now showed no feeling at all.

'That was a foolish thing to do . . . Mrs Henley. It's easy enough for a man to buy a woman in these parts, I suppose, but I figure a woman would have to go all the way to someplace like New York to buy herself a fancy man . . . if that's what you're lookin' for.'

He stepped around her and walked out of the saloon without a backward glance. He stopped long enough to roll a cigarette in the shade of the awning, and then he went straight to the Cowper house.

The judge was sitting alone on the shady front porch, but Beth soon joined him when she heard Halliday's voice.

As she slipped into the chair beside her uncle, Halliday was saying;

'I haven't told you what I think will happen next, Judge.'

'What do you mean, Buck?' Cowper asked.

'Henley will come back. And he'll have some gunman to back him.'

'Surely not!' Beth gasped.

'I reckon so,' Halliday said firmly. 'And it won't be long before he gets here.'

Cowper scrubbed a hand anxiously over his chin, shook his head despondently and asked tightly;

'Then there'll be more killing and more trouble?'

'Most likely so,' Halliday said, 'meanin' this town might still be able to use a peace officer that knows how to use a gun.'

Cowper nodded and said at once, 'The job is still yours, Mr Halliday, if you want it. All you have to do is say the word.'

'All right, Judge, that's exactly what I was hopin' to hear you say. I'll take it.'

Beth kept silent for a few moments, and then she said, 'What about the saloon job . . . Buck?'

'Mrs Henley can look after herself,' Halliday said, and he saw a gleam of satisfaction in Beth's eyes.

Judge Cowper was grinning broadly.

'I can have you sworn in today, if that's all right with you,' he said. 'By the way, what made you change your mind? You don't strike me as a man who does that very often.'

'I usually don't,' Halliday said as he looked straight at Beth.

The girl looked down at her lap, and her face took on a rosy glow that had nothing to do with the heat of the day.

An hour later, the new sheriff of Shimmer Creek pinned on his badge.

EIGHT

BASSETT'S BIG PLAY

Tom Bassett paced up and down relentlessly, cursing the heat, the hunger gnawing at his belly, and the buzzards that were circling with their eyes on the arroyo which held what was left of Ben Albert.

Jason Henley's temper was no better. He was tired of waiting for the stage and tired of watching Bassett.

'Why don't you settle down to wait?' Henley suggested reasonably. 'Marchin' up and down in this heat won't make that stage come any sooner, you know. Besides, you're driving me loco, just watching you.'

Bassett stopped and glared at him sullenly.

'You want to sit and stew in your own sweat, that's

up to you, Mr Henley! We're both waitin', and I guess we each have our own idea of how to go about it.'

Henley raised his eyebrows in surprise at the depth of Bassett's impatience. He decided this was not the time to push too hard.

'Ben Crowe will fix everything soon enough,' he said. 'Just see if he doesn't. All we have to do is wait for the stage to come. We'll just climb on board with Crowe and ride back to Shimmer Creek in style. Once we're there, it's just a matter of pointing Crowe in the right direction and standing back and watching.'

'All I can think of is Halliday, struttin' all over town while we sit here bakin' in this goddamn heat!' Bassett complained. 'Could be he's with your wife now, with her pleasurin' him just like she used to cozy up to all the rest of—'

Henley's stare hardened.

'What was that you said, mister?'

Bassett looked away.

'I'm right sorry I let that slip, Mr Henley,' he said. 'Didn't mean to.'

'Well, it did slip, all the same. You better tell me what you're talking about – right now.'

'Okay, I will. Your wife is the kinda female that just can't get enough of men, Mr Henley. She – ain't exactly particular about who she chooses, either. We never let on to you, because we figured you'd blame us more for tellin' you than you'd blame her for the way she is.'

Henley got up slowly and clenched his fists, shaking his head in denial.

'Damn you, Bassett, you're lyin' to me.'

'No, Mr Henley, it ain't a lie. It was Rafe that first got wise to her. But he got kinda scared when she wouldn't give him no peace and kept hangin' around him when he had work to do. I mean it when I say I'm sorry you found out like this, but hell, maybe it's for the best. She's been chasin' after just about everybody wearin' long pants, and that includes me . . . and now Halliday.'

Henley staggered back as if somebody had struck him. He sat down heavily and put his hands over his face. He stayed that way for a long time before he spoke again.

'Tell me you're lyin'. For hell's sake, tell me it ain't so. Maybe you're mad at me, or maybe it's just that the heat's got your head. Is that it?'

Bassett hesitated before he gave his answer, but he had no reason to fear Henley now, and he had no reason to sympathize with him either.

'It ain't a lie,' he said firmly. 'That woman of yours is just plain no good, Mr Henley.'

Suddenly, Henley lunged at him, and Bassett knew that he had gone too far. He scrambled back but Henley kept coming and Bassett lashed out with his fist in an attempt to ward him off.

Raving and snarling like a maddened beast, Henley bored in, smashing blow after blow into Bassett's face until his fists were covered in blood.

Bassett gave ground and braced himself so that when Henley ran at him again, he ducked and drove his shoulder into the man's chest.

Henley backed away as soon as he had his balance, but it was clear that he was only catching his breath.

Bassett had no desire to go after him, so he simply stood and waited with his hands hanging by his sides.

'Mr Henley,' he started to say, 'fightin' me ain't gonna change nothin', and I'm real sorry that it ain't.'

Bellowing like an enraged bull, Henley came charging in again. Shocked by the man's unstoppable rage, Bassett turned and tried to run, but Henley jumped onto his back and began to pound him viciously with his fists. It appeared that he could not stop himself. He was cursing and sobbing uncontrollably now, and his weight drove Bassett to the ground.

Bassett saw a rock just beyond his reach, and he squirmed forward, dragging both his own weight and the man on his back until his fingers closed on the rock. Gathering all his strength, he wrenched his body around until he was facing Henley.

He lashed out three times, and he got Henley in the face twice. When the man collapsed, Bassett pushed himself to his knees then got shakily to his feet.

Blood ran from the fresh gashes in his face, and his breath came in ragged gasps. He inspected his swollen fists and decided that one finger was broken.

Henley did not move for several minutes, and when he finally showed some sign of life, Bassett rushed in and kicked him in the head.

The sunset was turning the desert red now, and Bassett seemed uncertain what to do next.

'Hell, I didn't mean for all that to happen,' he complained. 'I was just so damn tired of waitin'. . . .'

Henley did not stir.

Bassett was telling the truth. He had not meant to beat up the man who had paid his wages. Once the fight started, he almost felt like he was up against Halliday, and that he was winning. Maybe that was what Henley had been feeling, too.

Bassett looked at the sky and lit a cigarette while he wrestled with the problem of what to do next.

It dimly seemed that everything could be put back just the way it was, if only he could be the one to put paid to Buck Halliday ...

Slowly, he mounted his horse and headed back to Shimmer Creek.

Buck Halliday walked the streets for half an hour after sundown and found no trouble.

The saloon was doing a solid trade. Halliday stopped in twice and each time he spotted Julie Henley somewhere in the crowd. For the moment anyway, she seemed to be interested only in the money which was rolling in.

He went to the livery and checked on the sorrel. He stroked the horse's nose and talked to it for awhile and then left instructions with the liveryman to give the horse extra oats.

After spending twenty minutes there, he retraced his steps through town.

He was passing the Cowper house when the door opened and Beth stepped out onto the porch. In the dim light coming from the house, Halliday could see her body outlined clearly in a graceful silhouette.

He had a mind to go up to the gate and speak to her, but instead, he went on by the house and headed for the saloon.

He had his hands on the swing doors when Tom Bassett limped into the saloon through the back door. The man looked like he'd been trampled in a stampede. His shirt hung in ragged strips, every inch of skin was blistered, bruised or bleeding.

Their eyes met across the big room, and Bassett spat out a curse and faded back into the night. Halliday ran after him, but when he reached the yard, it was empty and silent.

He stood listening with his hand resting on his gun butt until a shadow cut across the strip of light coming from the saloon.

Julie Henley was watching him from the back step. 'What is it, Buck? Is it Jason?'

'No, it's Tom Bassett,' he told her and shepherded her back into the saloon. 'He's out there somewhere. I sure thought he'd have more sense.'

'Are you sure it was him?' Julie asked. 'I can't believe he'd come back here, not after what you did to him. He might not be very smart, but I never would've said he was crazy as a loon.'

'It was Tom Bassett, all right, and he's one helluva mess. I don't know what happened to him after he left here, but it sure must've been bad. Whatever's goin' on, I reckon you should stay inside and clear the saloon. Tell everybody to get on home as fast as they can, Julie.'

Halliday closed the door on her as she continued to protest, and then he stepped back into the darkness of the yard.

He stopped several times to listen as he crossed the yard. He found Bassett's sweat-slicked horse hitched to the corner yard post and went past it into the alley. There was no sign of Bassett anywhere.

Halliday finally cut through the alley and came out onto Main Street. Men from the saloon were milling around with no place to go, clearly confused by the early closing. A few words from their new lawman sent them hurrying home.

The street finally emptied and silence settled again, heavy and oppressive. It felt like trouble.

Halliday made a full tour of the street, checking doorways on both sides of the street, and then he returned to the saloon and called for Julie. Nobody answered. He tried the door but it was locked. He hurried around to the back and called again. Still no answer. Maybe she was doing exactly as she had been told, but somehow he doubted it. She would have heard him call.

The back door was also locked, so he put his shoulder to it and smashed his way inside.

Going down the passageway to the barroom, he heard a scuffle of movement upstairs and then a muted cry. He bounded up the stairs three at a time and turned into the corridor just as Bassett burst out of Julie's room with Henley's little sneak gun in one hand and an untidy bundle of money in the other.

They saw each other at the same time, but Bassett was moving fast. He skidded down the hallway and tore open the door at the end that led to the upstairs balcony as Halliday's bullets peppered the plastered walls behind him.

Halliday pounded after him, but Bassett hurled himself off the gallery and dropped down to the yard below. When Halliday reached the railing, he could hear running footsteps scurrying away into the night.

Julie Henley was lying on the floor in her room when Halliday reached her. She groaned but did not speak as Halliday lifted her gently and placed her on the bed. He took a towel from the washstand to wipe the blood oozing from the deep gash on her forehead, and then he folded the towel into a pad and laid it over the cut.

Unable to help her anymore, he went downstairs and let himself out into the street again. Judge Cowper was there with Beth, with other people crowding around them.

'What's happening, Sheriff?' Cowper asked tightly.

'It's Tom Bassett,' Halliday said. 'He's back, and he just attacked Mrs Henley. Somebody needs to call the doc and see he gets to the hotel and back. Everybody else should go back home right now and stay there.'

'Perhaps we can help,' Cowper offered, and several men in the crowd nodded agreement. 'I think it's about time the men of this town did something to—'

'Look, folks,' Halliday interrupted, 'you're just makin' it harder for me if you hang around in the street. If there's shootin', I don't want to be holdin' back because someone might get in the way.'

That seemed to satisfy most people, and the crowd began to break up. The judge still stood his ground however, and his chin was raised in a look of stubborn determination.

'There's no time to argue this, Judge,' Halliday told him bluntly. 'It ain't safe out here.'

Beth nodded and put her hand on her uncle's arm. They started to move away, but then she turned back to Halliday and said;

'Do you think I could be of some help to Mrs Henley, Buck?'

Halliday seemed to consider her offer for a moment, but then he said, 'Let the doc do it. You two just get on home. You'll be safer there.'

Finally, the street was empty. Halliday stepped into a doorway and checked his six-gun. Then he settled back to wait. He knew that Bassett had come back for him, and he decided that the best thing to do would be to try and flush him out while the town was quiet.

Moving slowly and looking into every dark doorway, he went down one side of the street and came up the other. He was relieved to see that most folks now had their houses locked up for the night with the curtains drawn.

He was standing out front of the jailhouse when he heard a board creak. He stopped, strained his eyes and ears.

A minute passed. A tomcat yowled somewhere on the edge of town. A light wind started to blow, and the branch on an overgrown bush scratched against a window down the street.

Halliday made to turn away, but then he whirled and shoulder-charged the door of the law office, smashing it inward with such force that it tore loose from its hinges.

Halliday fell into the office on top of the door and

immediately rolled to the side.

He got just a glimpse of Tom Bassett before the bullets began to fly. He came up on his elbows to return Bassett's fire, and this time, he made no mistake.

Halliday's slugs seemed to tear Bassett apart. First the man's chest and then his neck, sending a fine spray of blood over the papers on the littered desk.

Bassett collapsed with his body arching into a spasm of pain and despair. The gun fell from his fingers and landed with a thump on the floor.

'Not yet, mister!' Halliday ordered. 'I want some answers before I let you go.'

'Let me go?' Bassett whispered. 'You mean that. . . ?'

'Sure I do,' Halliday told him, 'but first, you gotta tell me what Henley's up to.'

Halliday could see that Bassett was dying. There was so much blood on the floor now that he was afraid the man would not live long enough to answer his question.

'What's he doin'?' Halliday asked again.

'He's comin' for you,' Bassett croaked. 'Him and Ben Crowe. That's . . . all I know. Will you let me go now?'

Bassett's head lolled and his body went limp. Halliday released his grip and let him fall.

'Sure,' Halliday said. 'You can go . . . straight to hell.'

Wiping the blood from his fingers, Halliday glanced out the window fronting the street. It was still empty. He reloaded his six-gun as he continued to survey everything visible from the window, and then he slipped quietly through the doorway and propped the shattered door into the opening.

That would do till morning, he decided. Bassett would just have to spend his first few hours of the afterlife in the office of the Shimmer Creek lawman.

'Far as I know, he always was a loser,' Halliday said to himself as he started up the street.

Buck Halliday stood on the judge's front step, talking quietly until he was sure that Cowper could identify him. Finally, the front door opened just a crack and the judge said;

'Well, Sheriff?'

'Bassett won't cause anyone any more trouble,' Halliday answered calmly. 'He lived just long enough to tell me that Henley is comin' back, and he's bringin' Ben Crowe with him.'

'Who's he?' Cowper asked.

'A fast gun and a killer to the core. He'll take some stoppin'. I want to ask for your help now, before the action starts.'

Cowper frowned at him.

'Now you're asking for my help? Then why didn't you let me do something tonight?'

'Tonight was different,' Halliday said flatly.

'Tomorrow, I want the streets clear all day. Crowe travels by stage everywhere he goes. I need to know when the stage gets here.'

'It gets in around noon,' Cowper said thoughtfully.

'Then make sure everybody is off the street from about eleven o'clock. No exceptions, Judge. I don't want anybody in the line of fire except Ben Crowe and me.'

Cowper nodded, but then he added, 'Is that all you want us to do? Surely some of us could help you, especially since it sounds like Henley and Crowe will be in this together.'

'Henley doesn't worry me. I just want to make sure nobody gets in the way when I come up against him.'

Cowper nodded but he was far from convinced. 'There must be something more we can do.'

'Well, I went to see Julie Henley before comin' here,' Halliday said. 'She's hurt worse than I thought. I think somebody should stay the night with her.'

'I could do that,' Beth said over her uncle's shoulder.

'It could be a long night,' Halliday told her.

'It will be just as long wherever I am,' she said calmly. 'I – we – will be thinking about what's coming in the morning. I think you should let us take care of the town tonight, so you can get some rest.'

Halliday nodded.

'I'd be obliged then, Beth.'

'I'll get my things together,' Beth said and hurried off.

Cowper paced restlessly up and down the porch, occasionally glancing at Halliday. Finally, he said;

'I hope tomorrow is the end of it all, Sheriff.'

Beth came out of the house with a basket over her arm and gave her uncle a peck on the cheek.

'I'm ready,' she said to Halliday, and they went down the path side by side.

The doctor was still with Julie Henley when they arrived, and they went downstairs to wait in the darkened saloon. Finally, he came down the stairs, yawning widely.

'You look tired, doctor,' Julie said.

'It goes with the job,' he said. 'Most emergencies happen at night. Now I'm off to the Randall place to birth a baby. At least that's a happy event – much more satisfying than patching up damaged people. It's good that you can sit up with Mrs Henley, Miss Cowper. She's going to have a restless night.'

As Halliday let the doctor out the door, the man said, 'If everything goes well for Mrs Randall, I'll stop by first thing in the morning.'

Halliday and Beth climbed the stairs again, and Beth settled down in a chair beside Julie's bed. She did not look Halliday's way, but she could feel his eyes on her.

'Get some sleep, Buck,' Beth said finally, and he went quietly down the hall to the spare room.

He pulled off his boots and lay back on the bed. Within minutes, he was sleeping soundly.

NINE

NAME'S BEN CROWE

Dick Mason, the driver of the Layton to Shimmer Creek stage, nursed the team across the last of the desert stretch and hauled back on the reins. This was his regular run, and he had covered it so many times that he could almost do it with his eyes shut. The only thing different today was the buzzards. He had been watching them for a while now, and he could see that they were circling and dropping into a shallow arroyo. Leaning over the side so that the passenger could hear him, he hollered;

'We best check that out. You'd probably like to stretch your legs anyway. . . .'

The man inside glanced at the buzzards.

'Yeah,' he said. 'There's somethin' dead over there for sure.'

The stage creaked to a halt, and the passenger opened the door and stepped out stiffly, slapping the dust from his black clothes. He was lean to the point of being haggard, and none of the deep lines on his face suggested that they came from smiling.

He stopped to light the cigarette he had been rolling on the jouncing stage, and then he settled the gunrig more comfortably on his hips and started for the arroyo.

He was studying the telltale marks on the ground as he went – blood on a rock, hoof prints and foot-prints.

'See anythin', mister?' Mason called down from the high seat. 'We can't take too long or we'll be late. I ain't been late into Shimmer Creek in near on ten months, and that was only 'cause we run into a real bad storm.'

'This won't take long,' Ben Crowe said over his shoulder.

The driver sighed and checked his watch. He was on time so far, but he still had twenty miles to go.

Crowe nearly stepped on Jason Henley's battered body. There was no obvious sign of life, but Crowe squatted down and touched the artery on the neck. He felt a feeble pulse.

'Well,' he said, 'maybe you matter to somebody.'

He got to his feet and walked further into the arroyo. Buzzards flapped into the air, squawking and complaining at being disturbed. Crowe pursed his lips and went close enough to see what they had been feasting on. Then he returned to the mouth of the arroyo.

'There's one feller dead and another one in bad shape but still alive,' he said flatly.

Mason climbed down from the stage.

'Judas,' he said. 'There goes the schedule.'

He followed Crowe to the arroyo, and the gunman simply pointed down at Henley and folded his arms.

Mason was about to ask Crowe for help, but something stopped him before he mouthed the words. Cussing and grunting, he pulled Henley's limp body off the ground and started to drag him back to the stage.

Crowe went ahead and opened the door.

'Put him in the compartment,' he said, 'while I take another look around.'

'What about the dead feller?' Mason asked.

'I don't reckon there's enough of him left to bother,' the gunman shrugged, 'but that's up to you.'

'This here is a stagecoach, not a hearse!' Mason snapped, and then he climbed onto his seat and began to shave a fresh sliver of tobacco from his plug.

Crowe shrugged and sauntered back into the arroyo.

He returned a few minutes later but offered no information on anything he might have seen.

'Best drive on,' he said curtly.

'I sure won't argue with that,' Mason said as he waited for Crowe to climb aboard.

He had been thinking about telling Crowe that the injured man was Jason Henley, but he decided it was none of the gunman's business.

Gathering up the reins, he slapped them over the rumps of the horses and guided them back onto the trail.

Inside the stage, Crowe unceremoniously splashed water from his canteen over Henley's discolored face. Henley began to groan, but they traveled several miles before he finally stirred.

'Well,' Crowe asked with mild interest, 'what happened to you?'

Henley looked at him blankly. 'Where am I?'

'On the stage to Shimmer Creek. We found you a few miles back, real close to bein' buzzard bait. What happened?'

Henley tried to remember. His brow furrowed with the effort, and finally a gleam of enlightenment showed in his reddened eyes.

'Tom Bassett!'

'Who?' Crowe asked.

Crowe's toneless voice was beginning to annoy

Henley, but he said;

'Tom Bassett, he worked for me in Shimmer Creek – and when I find him, I'm goin' to kill him.'

'Reckon he has it comin',' Crowe said coolly.

'You could say that,' growled Henley, and for the first time, he realized that he was on a stage. He looked hard at Crowe, and finally asked, 'Who are you, mister?'

'Name's Ben Crowe.'

Henley tried to sit up and even managed what was meant to be a smile.

'Well, I'm Jason Henley,' he said, 'and I'm sure glad to see you.'

Crowe studied him thoughtfully for a moment before he nodded. 'I didn't expect to be met in this fashion, Henley. Seems your troubles are worse than you let on.'

'It's nothing you can't get me out of. I'm sure of that.'

'Let's find out about that,' the gunman said. 'What is it you want from me?'

Henley mopped his face with a stained handkerchief and reached for Crowe's canteen. He drank greedily then wiped his mouth.

'That's better,' he said gratefully as he handed back the canteen. 'Have you heard of a feller by the name of Halliday?'

'Buck Halliday?'

'That's him. I had Shimmer Creek just the way I wanted it until somebody sent for him. I had a pretty tough bunch working for me, too, but that bastard cut 'em to ribbons.'

Crowe folded his hands loosely in his lap and studied Henley with disturbing intensity.

Henley shifted uncomfortably under Crowe's intense gaze, and asked anxiously, 'Something wrong? You know this feller?'

Crowe nodded.

'Well, what about him?' Henley pressed.

'We locked horns once before.'

Henley brightened.

'Then I guess you've got more reasons than money to want him dead,' Henley said hopefully. 'All the better.'

Crowe shrugged and turned to look out the window. The country was sweeping past as the stage rocked along the trail, trying to make up time.

The full heat of the day was hammering down on the stage now, and the air that filtered through the curtains was hot as a furnace.

'I can't say I feel that way about it,' Crowe said eventually. 'But I wouldn't mind seein' him dead. As I recollect, he backed down the last time I came up against him.'

'He backed down from you, did he?' Henley grinned. 'Now ain't that music to my ears! So you called his bluff, and he backed down.'

132

'I sure wish you'd stop tryin' to put words into my mouth – if that's all right with you.'

Henley's mouth opened in protest, but then he caught the cold look in Crowe's eyes and simply closed it again.

Crowe stared blankly at the passing landscape. He was thinking about another place and another time.

Impatient though he was, Henley waited quietly for Crowe to speak.

'How far out of town do you reckon we are now?' Crowe asked so unexpectedly that Henley jumped in surprise.

Henley peered through the side curtains and said, 'About five miles, no more.'

Crowe reached up and knocked on the ceiling until he had Dick Mason's attention.

'Pull up, driver! Right here.'

Mason kept driving as he shouted, 'What in hell for? We'll be in Shimmer Creek in no time a-tall now. . . .'

'Stop here, I said!'

Mason leaned back on the reins and kicked the brake handle forward. The stage slewed to a halt.

Watching Crowe nervously, Henley licked his lips and asked, 'What you got in mind? You're not backin' out on me, are you? I'll pay you more if that'll make a difference. Just so you do the job.'

'Shut up,' Crowe told him fiercely, and then the

gunfighter stepped out of the stage and waved for Mason to join him.

Mason stayed on the high seat and spat a brown stream of tobacco juice over the side in preparation to speak.

'Mister,' Crowe said with quiet menace, 'this ain't some game we're playin'. Do what I say, and do it now.'

'I'm comin'!' Mason said hurriedly as he dropped over the side.

He stumbled but scrambled to his feet and stood watching Crowe nervously.

'We're gonna take two horses,' Crowe announced. 'It ain't far to town, and you'll make it fine. I'll need a blanket, too.'

'Mister, them horses ain't mine to give,' Mason protested. 'They belong to the Butterfield Overland Stage—'

Crowe's gun was in his hand. Neither Henley nor Mason had seen him draw – they only knew that the six-gun had been in the holster and now it was in Crowe's hand.

Mason nodded nervously.

'Okay,' he said. 'Okay.'

Crowe slid the six-gun back into leather and turned to Henley.

'Maybe you feel well enough to help him,' he said.

'I . . . I guess so,' Henley said uncertainly.

'Do it then, or we'll be here all damn day,' Crowe said, and then he leaned against the stage wheel and began to roll a cigarette.

Henley was furious. No matter how much Crowe was paid, he was still a hired man with no right to be giving orders to the boss. Much as he would have liked to say that, Henley kept stonily silent.

Nothing was as important as getting rid of Buck Halliday, and Crowe was the man for the job. Besides, Crowe scared him. The gunfighter was beginning to look very much like the kind of mad dog who wouldn't think twice about biting the hand that fed it.

It took all of ten minutes to unhitch two horses and rearrange the others in the shafts.

Both Henley and Mason were sweating and cussing before the job was done, but they kept their griping to themselves.

'What the hell's goin' on?' Mason whispered to Henley. 'Throwin' in with a feller like that sure ain't likely to win you any friends in Shimmer Creek, you know. From what I hear, your name is mud in that town already. This can only make it a damn sight worse. If you'll take my advice you'll—'

'Henley,' Crowe interrupted. 'Knock him out and throw him in the stage. Hobble that team so it don't run off before he comes to.'

Mason straightened and put up his fists, but Henley was making no effort to carry out Crowe's orders.

'What in hell for. . . ?'

'Just do it,' Crowe said, and although his voice was soft as ever, it was heavy with menace.

Henley turned and stared uncertainly at Mason.

'Maybe it's best to just do what he says,' Henley muttered. 'Hold still – and I promise I won't hit you too hard.'

Mason had heard enough. He reached down for the gun on his hip, but before his fingers even touched the butt, Crowe fired and the bullet tore into Mason's shoulder.

The driver staggered back against his stage, clapping his hand to the bloody wound, but then fury took over from the shock and he was reaching for his six-gun again.

This time, Crowe waited until Mason had the gun out of the holster. His second bullet nicked the weapon and sent it spinning off into space. As soon as it hit the ground, the gunman fired once more, shattering the butt plate and knocking the six-gun several yards further from its helpless owner.

The echoes died away while Henley and Mason stood there, gaping.

'Go get that gun now, Henley,' Crowe said tonelessly. 'And knock him cold, like I told you in the first place.'

Crowe stepped out of the scant shade of the stagecoach and sauntered forward with the arrogant ease of a man who had the world at his feet.

Mason simply stood there, with his hand clapped to his bloody shoulder again. He watched Henley dully as the man hurried to retrieve the six-gun with the broken butt.

Henley was on the way back when Mason muttered a curse and broke into a run.

It was Henley and not Crowe who gunned him down with his own bullet from his own gun.

The bullet hit Mason squarely in the back, and he fell facedown beside the horses in the shafts. The horses reared in their harness, and the stage started to roll.

Crowe coolly grabbed for the two horses who had been taken out of harness and held their heads.

Henley stepped forward far enough to grab Mason's foot and drag him clear of the nervous teamers. Then he turned him over and looked back at Crowe and said;

'He's dead.'

'I'd hope so,' Crowe said. 'You were no more'n ten feet away and his back was turned.'

The teamers were running now, and the stage rocked and rolled behind them.

'Told you to hobble that team,' Crowe said.

As they watched, the team veered off the trail. There was the sound of a distant crash as the stage struck a stump and toppled sideways.

Crowe appeared to lose interest and turned back

to the two horses he was holding by their bridles. He chose the smaller of the two and pushed the other toward Henley.

'Maybe you've been noticin' what happens every time you want to argue with me,' Crowe said in that soft, toneless voice. 'When we get to Shimmer Creek, mister, you just do what I tell you. No more and no less. Understand?'

'When we get there,' Henley snapped, 'all you have to do is take care of Halliday. I'll handle the rest.'

'Mister, you're a fool and a coward and a back-shooter and I don't like you. But since Buck Halliday is involved, I want to see this through. When we get to town, do exactly as I say.'

Henley was struggling to pull himself onto the broad back of the teamer. He was keenly aware that Crowe had given him the bigger horse and kept the only blanket for himself, to use as a makeshift saddle pad.

The big horse shied away from Henley again, and he turned to Crowe snapped irritably;

'Aren't you forgettin' who's payin' you?'

'You killed a man who didn't deserve to die, Henley. Maybe you are payin' me, but that sure doesn't buy my respect. Now let's quit all this jab-berin' and get ourselves into this town of yours.'

Crowe arranged the folded blanket on the horse's back and pulled himself up. He spent a con-siderable time getting the blanket just right before he was satisfied. He clicked his tongue, and the horse started forward.

Cursing under his breath, Henley did his best to follow.

Buck Halliday was up before first light. A few farm wagons were rolling into town already, but Halliday was sure he could rely on Judge Cowper to have the streets clear before the stage was due to arrive.

He brewed himself a pot of coffee in the rough kitchen in the back of the saloon and took it up the stairs with the fingers of his free hand through the handles of three cups.

Beth Cowper was still sitting by Julie Henley's bed, gently wiping the injured woman's face with a damp towel.

'How is she?' Halliday asked quietly from the doorway.

Beth looked back at him, and shook her head. Then she tiptoed across the room before she whispered, 'She had a bad night, but she's sleeping now. I think a few more days of quiet will see her back to normal. My, but that coffee smells good.'

'Yeah,' Halliday said. 'We can use it even if Julie can't.'

They stood in the hallway, sipping the hot brew.

'I hope she thanks you for this,' Halliday said. 'Now that she's restin' easier, I figure you should get on home. I can find somebody else to stay with her today.'

'I'd just as soon wait for the doctor,' Beth said. 'Then I'll go home and take a nap . . . you know, she's different than how I thought she was.'

'How?' Halliday asked.

Coloring a little, Beth said;

'She was so restless last night she talked a lot in her sleep. About the town, the worries she's had, her husband, other men.'

Halliday said nothing. There was a little silence, and then Beth spoke again.

'And she talked about you, too, Buck. She knew you saved her last night.'

'She's had a rough time,' Halliday said slowly, 'but she's brought a lot of her troubles on herself. She's just that kind of woman, Beth . . . if there's no trouble about, she'll go out of her way to stir some up.'

Beth was suddenly angry with him.

'Don't talk that way about her when she can't defend herself! It's not fair. I tell you, she has a lot of good in her, and given the chance—'

'Okay,' Halliday muttered. 'Thanks again for lookin' after her.'

On his way down the stairs, he wondered why it was that he could never have even a casual conversation with Beth Cowper without it ending in an argument.

Then his thoughts turned to Ben Crowe.

140

It had been years since he had seen the gunman, but he had no reason to think the man had slowed down.

Ben Crowe was damn good with a gun.

TEN

A LONG TIME COMIN'

It was past noon, and Buck Halliday was getting worried. From what he had heard around town, Dick Mason prided himself on keeping to a timetable, but for some reason, the stage today was well and truly late. Judge Cowper had been sure that the stage would roll in around noon, and now he was telling Halliday again that Mason was always on time.

Halliday shook his head and rested one foot on the judge's front step as they talked.

'Somethin' funny is goin' on,' he said. 'When Bassett came back last night, he'd been beat up worse than when he rode out. He ran foul of somebody – do you think it might have been Jason Henley?'

142

Cowper shook his head.

'Bassett's so old I'm certain he would be no match for Henley.'

'What if Henley met up with Crowe someplace outside town?' Halliday suggested. 'Let's say that Henley stopped the stage and Crowe was a passenger. That could explain why the stage is late. . . .'

'What are you getting at?' Cowper asked.

'I have a nagging feelin' that we're gonna get a visit real soon from Crowe and Henley, and you can bet your bottom dollar they won't come ridin' in on that stage.'

'Are you worried about going up against Crowe?' Cowper asked.

Halliday shrugged.

'Let me put it this way,' the judge pressed. 'Should we be worried for you?'

'There's no way a man can be sure about a gunfight, not until it's over,' Halliday said calmly. 'It's one man against another. One mistake, and it's all over. . . .'

'Doesn't it come down to how fast you draw?' Cowper asked, plainly disturbed more than he wanted to show.

'Up to a point,' Halliday said. 'Havin' your gun clear of leather is an advantage I always like to have. But Crowe's no slouch. It's been a long time since I saw him, but he's still alive. That stands for somethin'.'

143

Halliday seemed to be hesitating, and Cowper felt that he had something else on his mind.

He cocked his head to listen to the clink of glasses coming from the back of the house, as if he wanted to be sure that Beth was out of earshot.

'Like I said, Judge, you can never be sure until it's over. Men are just flesh and blood, and they can make a mistake or look away at just the wrong time. Guns ain't perfect, either. They can jam or misfire or just plain fall apart. I've seen it happen.'

'What are you trying to say?' Cowper asked gravely.

'If somethin' goes wrong, the important thing is to get Henley. Crowe's only interested in me. He won't want to tear the town apart just for the fun of it. He doesn't have a taste for that kind of thing. Probably wouldn't even do it on Henley's orders. Even if things go wrong, all you and your friends have to do is stay out of Crowe's way and get Henley. Don't forget that, Judge. You won't be able to help me, and you shouldn't even try. Understand?'

Cowper's mouth closed in a thin, tight line. He was considering Halliday's words as solemnly as he had ever considered any case when he was on the circuit. Finally, he said, 'But we couldn't let him get away with killing you. I've come to like you, young feller, but it's more than that. You're the law in this town now. There has to be respect. No one knows that better than me. . . .'

'When it comes right down to it, what happens between me and Crowe has nothin' to do with Shimmer Creek or the law,' Halliday told him. 'Crowe's wanted me for a long time. He didn't come all this way just for the money. He wants my blood. Now you just remember what I said. Give him a way out of town, and he'll take it. But get Henley. When it's all boiled down, he's the one to blame for every drop of blood spilled so far.'

The judge started to speak, but Halliday interrupted him.

'Just one more thing. Give Julie Henley a chance. Who knows, she might just make it with a business to run. That saloon could be just the thing she needs.'

With that said, Halliday shook the old man's hand and went on his way. He walked up the deserted main street and chose his spot outside the jailhouse. He could see all the way to the town limits and beyond to where the wasteland shimmered in the heat.

It was almost one o'clock when he saw two dark blobs wavering in the heat haze and growing steadily larger.

Jason Henley was hurting and sweating, but most of all, he was worried sick. Fear clawed at his stomach and left a sour taste in his mouth. He wanted to turn tail and run so bad that it felt like something was physically dragging at him, but he still wanted one thing more than his own safety. He wanted his town back and under his thumb.

Ben Crowe reined in slightly and waited for Henley to range up beside him. When the two teamers were plodding side by side, Crowe began to lay the whole deal out in that toneless, nerveless voice.

'The way I'll do it, Henley, is ride straight in and call Halliday out. By the looks of the empty streets, the town's expectin' us.'

Henley had wondered if Tom Bassett had come back to blurt out his story.

'Pay attention, mister!' Crowe snapped.

'I'm all ears,' Henley insisted. 'You say you want to go straight in? Isn't that a risk we don't need to take?'

'It's how it's gonna be,' Crowe said flatly. 'Halliday is no backshooter. I'll get my chance at him, and that's all I'll need.'

Henley dragged out his sodden handkerchief and mopped his brow.

The closer they came to the edge of town, the clearer it was that the town was waiting for them.

'After all that's happened,' Henley said carefully, 'there might be some folks in town who figure they've got guts all of a sudden. . . .'

'It'll be just Halliday and me,' Crowe insisted. 'That's how it goes, and we both know it. You just have my money ready. I'll want it as soon as this is over, and then I'll be on my way.'

Henley's eyes narrowed.

'No,' he said with all the firmness he could muster. 'I want you to stay around for a while, so I'll have time to get some more men. If you ride out and leave me with no one to back me—'

'That'll be your problem,' Crowe said, and there was a hint of feeling in his voice at last. 'I'll give this town back to you. What you do with it after that is up to you.'

He gave Henley an icy look as he added, 'There's only one thing that'd bring me back this way again – if I start hearin' stories that I was the one that killed that stage driver. . . .'

They were two hundred yards from the place where Main Street started, and Crowe could see one lone figure standing outside the jailhouse.

He pulled out his gun, checked it and dropped it coolly back into the well-oiled holster.

'Now git away from me,' he said absently to Henley, and the frightened man immediately veered away from him but followed at a distance.

Crowe's eyes were fixed now on that tall figure in the street.

He knew it had to be Buck Halliday, and he was completely immersed in the challenge.

Which man was better? Who had the luck today?

It was the great gamble. Ben Crowe lived for it. He knew full well that one day he would die for it. To Ben Crowe, the gamble was worth it.

Henley hesitated at the top of the street, and his eyes skimmed nervously along both sides of the boardwalk. There was absolute silence and nothing to suggest that anyone was holding a gun on him, but his belly still churned with fear. He dragged out the damaged six-gun that had belonged to Dick Mason, checked yet again to see that it was loaded and then held it down against his leg.

A tiny breeze came out of nowhere and seemed to travel right down the street, stirring a line of dust and then rattling against a derelict shack on the edge of town.

Henley reined in quickly and lifted his gun.

Crowe looked back at him and shook his head.

'Get a hold of yourself,' he said disgustedly. 'If they meant to cut you down, you'd be dead by now.'

Henley nodded agreement, but his nervousness remained and grew with every yard they advanced.

He would have liked to fire his gun at anything or nothing, just to relieve the tension.

It was not until he passed his own saloon and saw the doors shut tight that he began to feel hopeful. He nudged the horse into the shade of the overhang from which he had often surveyed his town.

When Ben Crowe drew rein in front of him, Henley stopped in the mouth of the alley which ran down the side of his saloon. He reached out and touched the side wall of the building as if it could give him comfort, or maybe courage. His head had been aching all the way from the creek, and now the pain was pounding so hard in his temples that it made him dizzy. Sweat ran down his face and under his collar.

For the life of him, he could not understand how Ben Crowe could go on looking like a man with nothing on his mind and no fear in his heart.

Then Crowe brought the horse to a halt and let the reins go slack. He was watching Halliday with interest, and Halliday was sizing him up with equal attention.

The only difference was that Halliday was watching Henley, too.

'Buck,' Crowe called suddenly, 'I reckon one of us has seen his last sunrise.'

Halliday straightened and stepped out into the harsh sunlight. He smoothed his hands down his shirt front.

Henley spotted the tin star on his shirt.

'They made him a lawman, Crowe,' he called hoarsely.

'I can see that. Why didn't you tell me?'

'I didn't know, but what difference does it make?'

'Henley,' Crowe said heavily.

'Yeah, Crowe?'

'Shut up.'

Halliday came slowly toward Crowe now, walking with the measured tread of a man who knew where he was going and why. He stopped fifty feet short of

Crowe and said, 'This town has nothin' against you, Ben. You're welcome to turn around and ride out with no trouble from anyone.'

Crowe dropped from the back of his horse and gave the animal a slap on the rump. He watched it until it disappeared behind the depot, then he turned his eyes back to the man he was here to kill.

Crowe showed Halliday something few others had ever seen – the ghost of a smile playing across those cold, somber features.

'This sure has been a long time comin',' he said. 'But here we are. Ain't that somethin'?'

'I'll say it again,' Halliday told him. 'The trouble in this town has nothin' to do with you. It's between Henley and the folks he's been fleecin'. And it's my job to protect them. I don't reckon either of us would dirty our hands with the kind of things Henley's been doin'. That's why we don't have a quarrel, Ben.'

'You're right about that, Buck,' Crowe said. 'To tell you the truth, Henley turns my stomach.'

'I guess you know he's payin' you with money he took from these decent folks.'

'You know the money doesn't have a thing to do with this,' Crowe said, and the grin widened.

Henley was down from his horse now and shifting impatiently from one foot to the other as he stood in the mouth of the alley. He strained to hear what was being said, but the two voices came to him only as a quiet murmur like the easy talk of two men sharing a drink or two at the end of a hard day.

He wanted it to be over. He felt like yelling at Crowe or maybe at the two of them to get on with it, but of course he didn't dare let out a peep.

'So what's this all about?' Halliday asked quietly.

'I thought you knew. It's about you and me.'

Halliday nodded and spread his feet. Ben Crowe's face went calm and still as a statue.

Henley knew that at last the time for talk was over. He gulped uneasily and checked the street around him. He saw that curtains were drawn back in almost every window, and he felt the weight of all those watching eyes.

He was so certain that the next sound he heard would be the roar of two six-guns that it took a moment or two to realize that footsteps were coming his way.

When he turned to look, Judge Cowper and four men from the town were tramping purposefully toward him.

Crowe flicked an angry look at Henley, and then he turned his face to Halliday and gave a slow, grim nod.

Halliday gave no sign of recognition, but his eyes were fixed on Crowe with deadly concentration.

The silence returned, and the tension held for one brief moment more.

Crowe's hand swooped in toward his thigh. His

right shoulder dipped slightly and his gun cleared leather. The gun came up in a blur, and now the gunfighter's cold eyes sparked with the fire of life.

For the briefest of moments, his lips parted in a smile.

Halliday had matched his draw, and both their guns rose together. The roar of a single shot ripped through the heat-seared silence.

Henley licked his lips and wrapped his sweating hands in the mane of the big horse beside him. He craned his neck and started to grin like a winner in a poker game when he saw Halliday bend until his hand touched the ground . . . but only to retrieve his hat.

Then he noticed something else – Ben Crowe's gun was falling to the ground.

Crowe still stood with his feet planted wide and there was no change in that stern, proud face.

For a fraction of a second, Henley wondered if his gunman had thrown his weapon down to show that the job was done.

Then Crowe stumbled sideways, as though attempting to restore his balance. His right leg buckled, and he went down on his knee. He still held his head high and his back straight, but something was very, very wrong.

It was only then that Jason Henley saw the blue-black mark on Crowe's neck and the blood welling out to stain the collar of the gunman's black shirt.

Crowe was down on both knees now like a man in fervent prayer, but the look on his face had nothing to do with faith. He could not believe that he had lost.

Halliday slid his gun back into the cutaway holster and headed for Crowe.

Judge Cowper and his friends were on the move again, heading straight for Henley.

Cursing and clutching the six-gun with the broken butt plate, Henley let the horse go and started toward the saloon, but he waited there on the boardwalk as if he could not decide which way to run. Then Cowper's voice came to him loud and clear.

'Your time's up, Henley.'

Henley dragged the swing doors apart, cursed and fumbled in his vest for the key to the storm doors. With his key in the lock, he turned and glared at the old judge. Until he fired, no one knew that he had his gun out.

The shot went wild, but it came close enough to the judge to make the old man step to the side and put his well-worn hunting rifle to his shoulder.

'He's yours,' Halliday called to Cowper without taking his eyes from the gunfighter just ahead of him.

Crowe had fallen onto his side, his face white with shock.

'Are you hit?' Crowe gasped.

'Only my hat.'

'Well, ain't that somethin'?'

'It didn't have to be this way, Ben,' Halliday said.

Crowe managed a tight smile.

'You know better'n that, Buck,' he said. 'Now listen close. About five miles outta town, you'll find the stage and the dead driver. Henley did that – shot him in the back. I don't want anybody sayin' I'd do a thing like that.'

'I'm obliged for the information,' Halliday said, 'but I would've known that wasn't your style without you sayin' so.'

'Yeah,' Crowe said weakly. 'I made a mistake, though. Don't know where exactly, but I done somethin' wrong. You should be the one that's dyin'. . . .'

The light went out of his eyes, and his body shuddered in a last, violent struggle for life.

It was too late to tell him, but Halliday said it anyway.

'You went wrong where we all did, Ben. When you first found out you were so damn good with a gun.'

People were edging out of the buildings along Main Street now, whispering and staring. Halliday saw the banker in the crowd and went to him and asked, 'Would you do somethin' for me, Mr Carrigan?'

'Yes, Sheriff, anything you ask!'

'I want you to give this to the judge. Tell him it

don't sit right with me.'

Halliday took the star from his chest and dropped it in the banker's hand.

'And one other thing,' Halliday said as the man began to move away. 'See that Ben gets a proper burial.'

'I will,' the banker said solemnly as he watched Halliday walk away.

Halliday pulled the broken door loose at the jailhouse and set it against the wall. He went inside only long enough to grab his saddlebag, and then he headed for the livery.

He was tightening the cinch on the sorrel when he heard a ragged burst of gunfire coming from the back of the saloon. The shooting stopped as abruptly as it had started.

Halliday swung into the saddle and guided the sorrel toward the back street.

'Mr Halliday! Mr Halliday!'

The banker was running after him, the tin star still in his hand.

'Was that Henley?' Halliday asked.

'Yes, it was,' the banker said. 'He's dead now . . . but he got his wife before the judge could stop him. Julie's dead, too.'

Halliday stared at the open range beyond the town limits.

'That's a damn shame,' he said. 'Julie had a lot of good in her. It was just that her luck was all bad.'

'I know,' the banker said heavily.

'Well, it's time for me to get goin',' Halliday said, but the banker came around in front of the sorrel, shaking his head.

'You can't just ride away like this, Mr Halliday,' he said. 'The judge wants to see you. A lot of people want to thank you for what you did. . . .'

'I've been paid in full,' Halliday told him as he edged the horse past and left the man staring stupidly after him.

'It will never be the same, Beth,' the judge muttered, looking down the street toward the jailhouse in the distance. 'He's left his mark here.'

Beth said nothing, but her eyes were brimming with tears.

Cowper turned to look her full in the face, and then he nodded and said, 'He left a mark on you, too, didn't he?'

Beth bit her lip and looked away.

'By hell, he did,' the judge said with a gush of understanding. 'Does he know how you feel about him, girl?'

Beth shook her head.

'He didn't want me, Uncle.'

'But did he know. . . ?'

Beth shook her head, her hair falling around her face.

'There was never a chance to tell him,' she said

jerkily. 'Not among all the shooting and fighting and . . . worry.'

'That's all finished now, Beth,' the judge said with more than a touch of pride. 'And this town still needs him. We'll all be sorry if we let him just slip through our fingers. . . .'

'What can I do, Uncle?' Beth asked. 'He just rode away. He's gone, and he didn't even bother to say goodbye.'

'A man like that never says goodbye to anyone,' the judge said firmly. 'That doesn't mean a thing. Now you listen, young lady. My horse is still saddled in the yard. You take it, and you go after that man. He's only been gone a few minutes, and if you hurry, you can catch him up at the river. When you find him, you say what's in your heart. Say it plain.'

'Do you really think I should?' Beth asked, and the judge heard the hope trembling in her voice.

'You'll never know by staying here talking to a foolish old man,' Cowper told her sternly.

Buck Halliday saw her coming and waited in the shade of a tree on the bank of Shimmer Creek. As she came near, she slowed the horse to a walk. Finally, she was close enough for him to take the horse's reins and help her down from the saddle.

Despite herself, the touch of his hands made her think of the night he had seen her naked and carried her to her bed. She could feel her face burning with shame – or was it excitement? All in a rush, she said, 'The town needs you, Buck.'

'But I don't need the town.'

'You're looking for something else then?' Beth asked, and she could not keep the disappointment out of her voice.

'I'm past lookin',' Halliday said. 'I've found what I want, but I don't know how I can keep it.'

Beth felt a tightness in her throat.

'Is it me, Buck?' she asked, shocked at her own brazenness.

'Yes, it's you. I knew that as soon as I saw what Mitchener and Shelton tried to do to you.'

Beth felt like her whole body was blushing.

'You mean you felt sorry for me.'

'That's not what I mean at all. I felt sorry for Julie Henley. It's somethin' else with you.'

'And what might that be?'

'A lot of things. Some of it's mighty hard to say.'

'Just try,' she whispered.

'You're brave and tough in any situation. You're kind and gentle, too.'

He stopped there, and Beth seemed disappointed.

'And you're enough of a woman to give a man everything he needs. I knew that the first time I saw you.'

'Oh,' she said, and she stepped into his arms and laid her head against his chest. 'I'm so glad you know that. I didn't know how to tell you, Buck. . . .'

Slowly, gently, she was pushing him back under the tree, where the grass was soft as a carpet. Then she sank to her knees and held his hands to pull him down beside her.

'Beth,' he said. 'There's somethin' else I have to say to you, and I better do it now.'

'Is it really that important?'

'I'm not comin' back to town with you.'

'I know that, Buck,' she told him calmly. 'One day you will come back to me, but not now.'

'Pretty lady, you sure are full of surprises,' he said.

'I know,' she said as she lay back on the grass.

'Is this really what you want?'

'Yes.'

The dew was settling and the stars were fading from the sky when the man and the woman reached contentment.

Silently, Beth sat up and began to smooth her hair back from her face.

Buck Halliday lay on his back, watching her turning back into the prim and proper person most folks thought of only as the judge's niece.

'I want you to go,' Beth said firmly. 'You're not ready to settle down yet. Trying to force you to stay would be worse than having a dog that runs away every time the gate is left open.'

'I know I've got my faults,' Halliday muttered, 'but

ain't you bein' a little harsh?'

'Not when I say I expect you to come back to me, just as soon as you are ready to stay,' she told him.

'You're somethin' special, Beth.'

'So are you, Buck Halliday,' she said as she stood up and gave her skirt a shake. 'But don't think for a minute that means I'm going to stand here crying while you ride off without a backward glance. I expect that's your usual style, but I'm going to give you something different to remember me by.'

'What might that be?'

'I'm the one that's leaving you behind,' she said as she lifted her skirts to climb into the saddle. 'I want you back, but not until you're all through wandering. Just you remember that every time some female feasts her eyes on you.'

'I will, Beth,' he said. 'That's a promise.'

'Good.'

He watched her ride off into the sunrise, and then he reached for his hat and his gunrig.

'You really are somethin' special,' he said again as he whistled up the sorrel.